Second Chance

C.L. Williams

authorHOUSE®

AuthorHouse™
1663 Liberty Drive, Suite 200
Bloomington, IN 47403
www.authorhouse.com
Phone: 1-800-839-8640

First published by AuthorHouse   4/7/2009

ISBN: 978-1-4389-3668-0 (sc)

Printed in the United States of America
Bloomington, Indiana

This book is printed on acid-free paper.

To Dee. Thanks for believing in me when no one else had the courage to do so. God couldn't have sent me a better sister.

ONE

THINGS WERE MOVING SMOOTHLY FOR Abrie Lofton. She'd had a long day at work but it was the third Friday of the month, which was "Girl's Night Out". That was always good news to her because she didn't see her friends often. Their schedules conflicted miserably, precluding them from doing their "girl thing" more frequently. It was already 7:00 p.m., which meant that she had only two hours to shower and get dressed. She'd need at least an hour to gas up and start the drive up the hill. The ladies had agreed to meet at 10:00 at the new night spot in Ravenwood, Pennsylvania. It was said to be posh and everybody who was anybody was going to be there, including players from the Steelers, the Eagles, and the 76er's. That kind of crowd would draw others who had careers or good jobs *with benefits*. Benefits were a must! There was nothing like dating a man who held a part-time job because that, more than likely, meant that he was living at home with his mama. "We don't want brothers who haven't already been raised," the club had agreed. This "club" was comprised of five ladies who had had enough of the junk that the world of poor, inconsiderate, lazy, shiftless men had to offer. They had decided that they wanted husbands and they were on a mission to find them. Two of them had been married before. The others had never had that experience, and matrimony seemed more fascinating and exciting to them than it really was. One of the women had lost her husband to cancer and desired male companionship, but was a little gun shy after watching the disease suck the life out of the man she loved. "It was a rough experience," she reported, "that was not anything that anyone should have to go through twice."

"Girl, it's time to get gussied up! Ravenwood, get ready cuz here I come," Abrie told herself aloud. The water was running in the shower and her clothes were laid out on her bed. In spite of the early preparations, it took the full two hours for her to get dressed and she still needed time to put on her make-up. Halfway, through her time limit, her phone rang.

"Greg. Hi," she said as she rolled her eyes. "I told you that it just wasn't working. I tried but things are just not the same. Please don't put yourself through this anymore. For that matter, leave *me* out of it. I've done all that I can do. She says she doesn't want to be with you anymore. I can't help you. You should have thought about that before you did what you did."

Greg was sobbing on the phone. He was the estranged husband of one of the girls in the club. Della didn't want to have anything to do with him after he drained their checking and savings accounts and ran off with his secretary. After six months, he realized that the grass was not greener on the other side. He tried to come back but Della would not hear of it.

"Greg, I've got to go. I'm running late. If you want my advice, just give it up. There is no chance of reconciliation and, if you ask me, I wouldn't get back with you either! Not after what you did! Let it go, man. Get over it. I'm sorry, I can't help you...No, I won't talk to her for you...Goodbye, Greg."

She had already showered at the time of the thirty minute phone call but had not gotten dressed. By the time she hung up, she was rushing to get dressed and as always, the shoes were not quite the color she needed so she had to spend some time finding the right pair. This night was going to be the night. Abrie could feel that this time was going to be different. Tonight *was* the night. She found her shoes and looked at the clock. It was 8:45 and she needed to fix her hair. That was certainly going to take some time but she wasn't stressing. She knew of a shortcut up to Ravenwood. It was kind of dark but it would be okay. It was a back road but it would cut off about ten minutes of the travel time.

At 9:05 exactly, Abrie grabbed her keys and ran out the door. She started up her Honda Accord and headed for route 95. Traffic heading toward 95 was steady but not bad. The main thoroughfare was backed up which was odd for that time of evening. She had decided that the back road would have been the most viable alternative, whether she was running late or not. She was really looking forward to the evening. She reached down to turn on some music and found one of her favorite CD's. She hit the play button and waited for what she called her theme song to come on and she sang along--Loudly...

"Freak me, Baby. Aw, yes. Freak me, Baby. Just like that..."

She sang along with the group, "Silk", while sifting through the make-up bag on her lap. She was used to putting her make-up on in the car since she did it every morning as she drove to work. She opened her compact and began rubbing powder on her face. She groped around in the dark to find her eye pencils. Suddenly she saw bright lights flash in her face.

"Sorry," she laughed as she swerved to get back into her lane. Route 95 was a long, winding two lane hi-way that not many people used during the evening hours. It was generally used by truck drivers which made it a little unsafe to travel at night. Her mother constantly warned her about taking that road, often saying that she got a funny feeling every time she even saw that stretch of pavement. She urged Abrie not to use that road but Abrie just felt that her mother had become paranoid in her old age.

"Let me do all the things you want me to do..."

Just as Abrie was getting into the song, which was playing for the second time, she dropped her eye pencil and began tapping the floorboard of her car with her foot to find it. No luck. She searched some more with her foot, coming up with nothing. She perused the road and saw no lights or cars coming so she bent down to search with her hand. The next ten seconds seemed like hours to her as she heard the sound of the tractor trailer's horn and peered out the windshield. She saw that she was directly in front of the semi and tried to swerve out of its way but overcorrected and hit the ditch on the other side of the road. Her car spun out of control and seemed to roll and roll and roll. All she could hear was the sound of breaking glass. She could feel things in her car flying around and most of all, she felt her body jerking. The car finally stopped moving and the smooth rhythmic sounds of the group "Silk" could still be heard playing for what seemed like a long time. Suddenly she felt cold. Then there was darkness.

TWO

THE "JANE DOE" HAD BEEN in the morgue since the evening before. Marlena Paterson was lost in thought. She began to wonder about who was looking for his daughter or her sister or, God forbid, his mother. "Jane" looked to be in her early twenties. "Such a tragedy," she heard herself aloud as she signed the forms releasing the body for further investigation. As the chief coroner, she had seen quite a bit of tragedy in her many years of investigative work but this one struck her differently; almost as if it were her own daughter. She found herself studying the young face and wanting to cry. She wanted to cry for the mother of this lifeless victim. She wanted to cry for her own children because young people were so reckless and didn't seem to care about whether or not tomorrow would come, let alone carefully plan a future. She had three "young people" of her own and praise God, they were all grown. The youngest was 23 years old. She felt blessed to have reared them well, in spite of the fact that she was a single mother for the majority of their childhood. Her husband, their father, had perished in a motorcycle accident which spearheaded her career in the coroner's office. She had never seen anything in life so mangled and had much difficulty identifying the body.

She felt a tear roll down her face and tasted the salty liquid as it circled the corner of her upper lip. Startled by the fact that she was crying for this person who she didn't know from the man in the moon, she wiped her face and patted the makeup underneath her eyes in a gesture to regain composure before leaving the examination room. Still, she felt a tugging on her spirit and a real need to cry. She didn't understand the intensity of the emotion she was feeling because she hadn't cried in years for the lifeless bodies that filled up her work docket. The neophytes cried for them; not the veterans. She walked briskly to her private office, striving to get inside and close the door before the tears began to roll down her face again. She made it inside but only seconds before a river of tears forced its way down her face. Not understanding what was happening, she wiped the tears and began to bury herself in paperwork as an attempt to deny the experience. Marlena had a lot of pride and would never admit that she still felt a connection to people after all of these years. Desensitization was the key to success in this business and the best way to achieve that was to avoid any feelings brought on by what you saw rolled in on the gurneys. Death and bodies were her business and no good coroner personalized what he or she saw. Death, after all, was a part of life that happened everyday and no one really knew how they'd meet it; car accident, gunshot, boating accident, heart attack, etc., and a good coroner was not surprised by anything he or she saw. At least if he was, no one knew about it.

Marlena had an urge to call home but shrugged it off figuring that no one was there. She had remarried and her husband was out with the boys. It was his night to bowl and none of her children lived at home. It was going to be a long night and if she were to get any work done, she was going to have to rid herself of the emotion as well any urge that was not work related.

Ross Paterson was involved in his bowling game. He was having a blast with his buddies and coworkers. He had put in a long day at the office and his wife was working the late shift so he had put all of his worries and concerns aside as he always did when he bowled. But this evening, around 9:35 p.m., he broke out into a cold sweat. He also felt a little dizzy with some queasiness in his stomach. He had just thrown a spare and was walking toward his seat. He'd hoped no one had noticed because he wasn't ready to go home and figured that he'd just eaten something that didn't settle well with him. He figured he'd sit and rest for a few minutes and whatever it was would soon pass. He was right in his prognosis but didn't anticipate the heaviness of the thoughts that would ensue. The moment he sat down, he was met by an intense desire to call his wife. Puzzled, he sat for a few minutes and endured it. After having sat for a while, he excused himself and went looking for a telephone.

"Mrs. Paterson, your husband is on line three," a voice said over the speakerphone in her office.

"Thanks, Robin. Hello, Ross," she said as she picked up the receiver.

"Hi, Babe," he returned. "Is everything okay?"

Very dryly and sounding annoyed, she answered, "yeah. Why do you ask?"

"I'm not sure. You were on my mind in an unusual way," he came back timidly.

"Oh, really?"

"Yeah. Like something was wrong. I was concerned and had to call."

"That was sweet of you but things are fine here. How's the bowling game?" She sounded as if she wanted to placate him with an inquiry about his world.

"It's going well but are you sure you're okay?"

"Everything is fine but if I don't get off this phone with you, I am going to fall behind in my work and I'm not going to be okay. I'm going to need help and if you're not up for the task, I suggest you let me get back to what I was doing," she snapped.

"Well, okay, but if you need me you can page me..."

"Okay. Enjoy your game," she interrupted.

"Babe."

"Yes, Ross."

"I love you."

"Uh-huh, me, too. Bye," she said dryly as she hung up the phone in his face.

Ross didn't take the coldness personally. He had been with his wife for more than ten years and he knew that her passion for her work caused her to take life very seriously. He knew to give her the space she needed and to never, ever nag her about the way she chose to express her emotions. It wasn't always like that. Usually she was short and dry when it was time for her to take a much needed vacation, but getting her to take the time off was like pulling teeth. It was as if she felt that the coroner's office couldn't and wouldn't function without her. Sometimes she did seem a little self-absorbed but you would never hear that slip out of Ross' mouth. He loved his wife and would never say anything negative about her. He loved her and she knew it because he told her every chance he could, through words and/or actions. He was a very loving husband but he had to be. He had to compensate for what was not found in abundance in their home. Not now or ever before--at least that he knew of.

THREE

"THAT'S JUST LIKE BRIE. THAT tramp stood us up. She probably met Mr. Right on the way here and decided that she'd get a jump start on tonight's mission, I guess."

"Oh, quit it," Della said to China who had just spoken. "You know that Brie is always late. That girl will be late to her own funeral. Can't you see it? 'We're sorry, Reverend. This is just like Brie. She is always late. None of us are surprised. It's been this way all of her life and none of us expected it to change with her death.'" The four women were almost paralyzed with laughter.

"Oo-wee. Look, look, look," China said as she drew everyone's attention to the tall, well-built brother who was approaching their table. As if rehearsed, the ladies, in unison, gave the affirmative "um-hmm". This one looked as though he were an Atlanta, Georgia import. The dead give-away was the enticing "corn-fed" look, as the ladies described it. He was built solid like a Mac truck, his skin was as smooth as silk and his teeth were as white as pearls. He was definitely good for an evening or two if nothing else. He didn't have to talk. All you wanted to do was look into those dreamy eyes of his and be swept away by his incredible smile.

"Good evening, ladies," he said as he passed by. At that moment, the ladies realized that none of them were talking because they were all staring with their mouths open at the "tall drink of chocolate milk" that was walking by. No one spoke back. They were absolutely taken by his beauty. He smiled and nodded as he strolled--more like pranced-- by.

As he passed the table, the ladies noticed together the glutes that the man was packing. They were all ready to pounce on him at once but thought better of it. Maybe the real reason no one went for it was because they couldn't move. Silence engulfed the table for the 30 second delayed reaction that preceded the sighs and comments that came out in confusion as they all talked over one another. It was clear that they were all in agreement that he was "ultra-fine".

"That is a 'Brie specialty'. I'm glad the heifer is not here because I don't know that I would have been able to sit still as she snagged that one," Nancy confessed. The others laughed and nodded their heads in agreement.

"By the way, where is the cow?" Everyone turned and looked at Patricia, who never used those "terms of endearment" like the others. A burst of laughter caused her to blush.

"I think we have a convert here," laughed China. "The Reverend Boutier is going to faint if he ever finds out that his sweet preacher's kid has used the word 'cow' in reference to one of the sheep of his flock."

Another burst of laughter brought the women to near paralysis.

"I'm going to call Brie to find out where the hell she is," said Della as she pulled her cell phone from her purse. She dialed the number and got Brie's voice mail. "Tramp, we're all here waiting for you. Where are you? We've already picked out your husband. He walked by the table and I'm telling you, I swear I saw your name tattooed on his chest. Hurry up before someone else snatches him up."

The ringing of the phone drew the attention of the truck driver to her purse. He had gotten to the car, saw the unconscious woman and pulled her from the wreckage. The car was banged up pretty badly but, fortunately, he was able to pull her out of it. He could see that she was breathing and it was a good thing that she had been wearing her seat belt. He had radioed for help and he knew that it was on the way. Her purse had been thrown a few feet from the car and the sound of the phone ringing gave him an idea. He took the phone out of the purse and returned the call.

"Where the hell are you?" Della said as she answered her phone.

"Ma'am, my name is Dirk Ramsey..."

"What the hell are you doing with my friend's phone you son of a..."

"Ma'am, there's been an accident and your friend is hurt..."

"Oh, my God," Della screamed drawing the attention of a few people who were standing nearby. "Brie's been hurt. Oh, my God! Oh, my..."

"Ma'am you have to listen. I need to tell you where we are."

"How do I know that you're not trying to pull a fast one on me? This is not funny, Mr. You had better be..."

At that Della, who had left the table in the noisy club with the others right behind her, heard the piercing scream of the sirens.

"Do you hear that? I'm not trying to do anything to hurt anyone. I'm trying to help. The ambulance and the state troopers are here now. Listen carefully as I tell you where we are."

"Let me speak to an emergency professional," she insisted.

After what seemed like ten minutes of silence, a woman identified herself as a state trooper and gave Della their whereabouts. Hysterical, Della began trying to describe to the others what had just happened. The women left the nightclub in a hurry, piled into their cars and headed for the scene of the accident, which was only twenty minutes away. By the time they got there, Brie, still unconscious, was in the back of the ambulance. One of the paramedics was shutting the doors while another was administering paramedical procedures.

Nancy, the calmest of the group, had been finding out pertinent information from the emergency professionals as the others were trying to get to Abrie. The truck driver had given her his best account of how the accident had happened. The paramedics let her know what hospital she'd be taken to and she in turn gave necessary information to the troopers. After taking care of the business, Nancy had a scary thought: Marlena Paterson. What would Mrs. Paterson think? How would she handle this one? She'd have to experience some kind of emotion, and *that* would probably kill her. She was so sterile, so void of emotion and had been for the five years Nancy had known her. This woman was an ice princess and honestly, there was little doubt that something as tragic as this would crack her.

The sound of the ambulance starting up brought Nancy out of the zone she'd gone into and she joined the other women, who, at this time, were wailing as if Brie had died. Somehow, Nancy knew she'd be okay.

FOUR

Marlena found herself staring into space. She could not focus on her work. Frustrated, she threw her pencil across the desk and cursed under her breath. She got up from her desk and proceeded toward the examination room where Jane Doe's body lied cold and stiff. As she walked down the corridor, she began to feel alone and cold. The corridor seemed more like a tunnel and there was no one in sight. She wondered where her coworkers were and before she knew it, she was standing in the doorway of the examination room. Jane Doe's body was there underneath a sheet. Marlena walked over to it and stared at it for a minute. She pulled the sheet off the woman's face and was shocked at what she saw. She had to do a double take because the woman looked so much like her daughter, Abrie. At that moment she realized that it had been a while since she last spoke with her youngest child.

"It hasn't been *that* long," she said to herself aloud. "I talked to her on..." Her mind drew blank. It had indeed been a long time. She couldn't remember the last time they'd spoken, and vaguely remembered the gist of the conversation. "Well, the girl *is* grown. I don't need to talk to her every day. She'll never learn to be independent if I continue to treat her like a small child. I'll call her tomorrow."

"I've just been informed that a family is coming down to ID the body," said the medical examiner who was assigned to the case.

Startled by the sound of the voice but careful not to show it, Marlena turned around to face the young woman who had just entered the room. "What do you know about this one so far?"

"Well, there's definitely been some foul play." At that, the woman completely removed the sheet from the body. She pointed out three gunshot wounds in the lower back and abdomen. "Looks like she was shot first in the abdomen and turned and tried to run but her assailant shot her twice more after that. There is skin and hair underneath her fingernails so there's evidence of a struggle. The toxin levels in the body are real high, suggesting the administration of some type of chemical. We're running tests right now to see if these were street drugs or some type of poisoning but, nonetheless, this definitely appears to have been a homicide."

Marlena turned around slowly and walked toward the door. She felt a piercing in her stomach, then dizziness and a little faint. She reached behind her and grabbed the edge of the gurney, pushing it slightly forward as she broke her fall.

"Marlena, are you okay?" the young medical examiner asked.

"I'm alright. I think it's hot flashes. I'm starting to feel my age," she said and started toward the door again. This time she made it out but headed straight for the restroom, barely making it into the stall before throwing up. She decided to go home but not because she was sick, she'd later rationalize, but because she had vomited on her clothing.

Upon returning home, she saw a couple of cars parked in front of her house that she didn't recognize. She also saw a couple that she *did* recognize. They happened to belong to a couple of her daughter's friends. She wondered what was going on. Had Abrie come home and brought some friends with her? As she pulled up in the driveway, she saw her front door fling open. Ross came running out acting very strangely. Not long after she put her car in park, she found out the answers to her questions.

"Sweetheart, there's been an accident and Abrie is in the hospital. We have to leave now and go and see about her," Ross blurted out.

"What are you talking about? Calm down," she scolded. At that time, a state trooper approached her to answer any questions. Marlena looked at the officer and began talking shop! "So there's been an accident, huh? One car, two cars or a pile up?"

"There was only one car involved, Ma'am".

"Blow-out, spin-out, over-correction, speeding, what?"

"It seemed to have been an over-correction. There was an eyewitness at the scene. But your daughter..."

"You've told my husband where we can find her, haven't you?" she interrupted.

"Yes, Ma'am."

"Well, thank you for all of your assistance. We will take it from here."

Everyone, including the state trooper, stood by astounded. No one moved for the next few seconds except Marlena, who proceeded toward the front door. Ross, who was nearly hysterical by this time, followed her into the house. The state troopers left.

Inside the house, Della and Nancy were nervously pacing the floor and as Marlena entered, the two women froze. Marlena breezed by them en route to the master bathroom to shower. Though she barely noticed them, she did greet them. Ross came in and nearly collapsed.

"China and Patricia are already at the hospital and we are on our way," said Nancy after her.

"I'm on my way. What hospital is it?" she asked.

"Bay View General," Nancy responded.

"How many times have I told that girl not to travel that road? A hard head makes a soft behind. Thank God she's alive. I'll meet you all there later because I need to take a shower. Would you do me the favor of dropping Ross off? I'm sure he's ready to go now and if she's conscious, she'll want to see him."

"Sure, Mrs. Paterson," Della said.

"Thanks," she said from the top of the stairwell and disappeared.

Della, Nancy and Ross started toward the door without saying a word. Ross was a nervous wreck and desperately needed some consolation. The three of them walked to the car arm in arm, got in and drove to the hospital. The complete silence made the fifteen minute drive seem like hours. Each of them wondered what the other two were thinking, if they were alone in their thoughts and whether or not now would be a good time to discuss any of it. Thinking better of all of the above, they all sat quietly. When they got to the hospital, they were told that Brie was being "tended to by the finest" in Pennsylvania. They found out that she was being examined and had not regained consciousness. Afterwards, Della, Nancy and Ross joined China and Patricia in the waiting room. After several minutes of silence, Ross fell apart.

FIVE

All Abrie could feel was cold. Though the light in the room was very bright, she didn't recognize where she was. She felt a real sense of peace which led her not to care too much about her whereabouts. She liked what she was feeling and sensed movement around her but couldn't see anyone. It felt as if there were people around her but her eyes wouldn't focus on them. Strangely, it felt good. She tried to speak but couldn't. Then all of a sudden, it seemed as if something grabbed her, removed her from the place she'd been enjoying and began to suffocate her. She couldn't breathe. She tried to fight but couldn't due to the "thing" that had her in its grasp. She attempted to scream but nothing came out. She struggled and struggled but wasn't moving on her own. It seemed as if this "thing" had sucked all of the power out of her. She wanted to cry but couldn't. She wanted to run but couldn't feel her legs. The peace was replaced by fear and anxiety--intense fear and anxiety. She seemed to be losing oxygen and that scared her even more. Never before in life had she felt so helpless. She didn't know what to do but what did it matter? Everything she tried to do up to this point proved fruitless. "God, help me," she thought to herself. "Please, God, help me."

Suddenly, as quickly as it began, the terror ceased. Still, she could not talk or move. She didn't understand what was going on. Then, a chill rose against her body and the light started fading as if controlled by a dimmer switch.

The doctor appeared in the waiting room in search of the loved ones of Abrie Lofton. The news he had wasn't good but it could have been much worse. All he could tell them was that she was still unconscious but her brain activity was stable and her vitals were good, considering the trauma she'd suffered only a couple of hours before. "At one point, she seemed to be responding to our efforts but we were not able to bring her out of the coma."

"Coma?" Ross asked.

"There seems to be extensive internal injuries. Although she was wearing her seatbelt, it appears that she was not wearing the harness properly, allowing her upper body to make contact with the steering wheel and not protecting her from the jolting her body went through."

"Is she going to die?" China asked the doctor candidly.

"It's too soon to tell. We don't yet know the extent of the injuries but we will do the best we can." With that, he turned and disappeared into the hospital corridor.

Ross sat down and buried his face in his hands. The four ladies sat quietly shedding tears for their friend. It was 1:30 a.m. and Marlena Paterson had not made it to the hospital. Though he said nothing, Ross' fury was felt throughout the room.

At home, Marlena had decided to brew some fresh coffee and take a look at the day's newspaper. As she waited for the coffee to finish, she took a moment to relax in her favorite easy chair. It was the smell of vanilla beans that assisted her as she drifted off to sleep. The ringing of the phone awakened her.

Ross' fury could be heard all over the hospital waiting room as he shouted into the phone at his wife. "Where the hell are you? Why aren't you here yet? Don't you care that our daughter is lying in an emergency room with her fate hanging in the balance?"

"Ross Paterson! As long as we stay married, don't you ever speak to me in that tone! Who do you think you are?"

"Perhaps that's been the problem. I lost who I was ten years ago but now I am going to show you who I am! I am the man in this marriage and I've had enough of wearing the skirt and pantyhose. I am sick and tired of making excuses for your irresponsible and apathetic behavior. You'd better get yourself to this hospital in a hurry. If she dies on that table and you're not here, you'd better be out of the house before I get home and I mean this more than anything I've ever expressed to you before!"

At that, he slammed down the phone.

Ross' reaction served as the catalyst to the wave of emotion that broke out between the loved ones of Abrie Lofton. Patricia got up and ran out of the emergency room. China got up and ran after her. Nancy and Della stayed to tend to Ross. Though it was never discussed, the two women secretly cheered as Ross Paterson stood up to his wife for the first time that any of them knew about.

The truth of the matter was that the marriage was falling apart because Ross had absolutely had enough. He was tired of the lack of affection for him as well as for the children in the family. Ross hadn't been able to have children of his own so when he met and married Marlena, her children became his children. He loved them as if they were his own but she simply refused to allow him to adopt them. For years he felt as if she were holding on until her late husband, Reggie Lofton, came back. She never fully accepted the fact that he had died in that motorcycle accident. As a result of her denial, she withheld the love and affection due her children as well as her husband. She also cheated herself out of the love they wanted to give her and refused to love herself. It was as if they'd all been imprisoned by her loss. From time to time Ross would ask himself why he married her but resolved that the kids needed him, so he elected to stay there. The three children often showed their love and appreciation for him. He knew they loved him and that was enough to make him stay with the family. But today was the day to exert his manhood and to reclaim the authority usurped from him ten years ago. Honestly, he loved Marlena and didn't want to leave her but things had to change. This rage had been building up for sometime but Ross, being the docile individual everyone knew him to be, couldn't find the right time or place to do it. After seeing his "baby" hurt like that and get no support from her mother, Ross had had enough.

Surprised at his demeanor, Marlena found herself hanging up the phone and returning to her comfortable position. She'd never seen Ross like that before and quite frankly, didn't know he had it in him! Truth be known, she really needed Ross to stand up and be the man but she'd gotten away with too much for too long. The problem was that now, she was accustomed to running things in the marriage. She wasn't sure how she was going to deal with him when she got there but she knew that she couldn't just let this go. If she did, he would spin out of control and she wasn't having that. Oh, no! If he wanted to be the man, he should have done it years ago. Reggie would have never allowed things to go this far. In fact, she would have never stood up to "Reg", the way she did to Ross.

Reggie stood about 6'5" tall and weighed around 275 pounds, taking no lip from anybody. He didn't have to say a confirming word about that because it was understood by anyone who'd seen his facial expression. It seemed that he was constantly frowning. He was a very, very serious man who didn't say much more than he had to, unless you made him angry. If you made him angry, you had to pay dearly, catching it for everyone else who'd crossed him before he blew and when he blew, everybody knew. Not even Marlena could calm him down when he erupted.

Marlena loved Reggie and he loved her more. He was her first love and they'd dated for several years before they married and had children. They met at a blues festival one year and sparks flew the moment they laid eyes on each other. Many say that it was a match made in Heaven. There was nothing he wouldn't do for her; nothing except refuse to purchase and ride the motorcycle on which he met his demise. She begged him not to buy "that stupid thing", but his friends encouraged him to do it anyway. She often stood on the opposite side of issues from his friends and usually he'd listen to her, but this time they won out. She was sick when he pulled up on the shiny motorcycle one Friday afternoon. When she saw it, she was outraged. "Reg, what did you do?" she asked frantically. "Please tell me that this is not yours!"

"Woman, can't a man have a little fun for once in his life?" he asked as if to minimize her concerns.

"But Reggie, you know how I feel about this," she cried.

"Woman, go and fix my dinner. The boys will be here in a couple of hours," he said as he shooed her into the house.

Unbeknownst to her, the "boys" and Reggie had planned a weekend ride and her husband was preparing himself for it. They were scheduled to leave that evening and to return the following Sunday, but Reggie never returned. Marlena remembered feeling a piercing in her stomach, then dizziness and a little faint!

Suddenly it hit her. That was the same feeling she'd experienced earlier that evening before coming home from work. Abrie must have been having her accident as she was looking at the Jane Doe in the examination room! Marlena jumped straight up from her chair and ran upstairs to get dressed. She felt the need to get to her baby. She needed to get to the hospital. Maybe, just maybe, she could help this time. She was, after all, a doctor. She got dressed, jumped in her car and sped to the hospital. On the way there, she began to reminisce, as if being shown a "this-is-your-life-tape". She remembered Abrie's first step, her first missing tooth, her first slumber party, her first date, etc. The tears streamed down Marlena's face like a river. She found herself really sobbing by the time she reached the hospital parking lot. In fact, she was screaming. "Why, why, why, Lord? Why did you let him die? I prayed and asked You not to let him buy that stupid motorcycle but You did not answer my prayer! You didn't hear me! Why did you have to take my husband away from me?" She banged her head against the steering wheel of her car a few times. There were people in the parking lot staring at her but she didn't care. For the first time in years, she just didn't care. She was grieving and it didn't have to be a pretty sight. She was mourning but not because of her daughter's accident. It was if she had been given a second chance to mourn the death of her husband.

SIX

JUST OUTSIDE THE EMERGENCY ROOM exit, Patricia sat sobbing with China attempting to console her. Patricia couldn't bear the possibility of losing her friend. Brie had been there to help her through many a problem. Being raised a preacher's kid, it wasn't easy to talk about your problems with others without being judged. There was definitely a double standard. It was as if others felt perfection was a part of the benefit package associated with doing God's work. The adults who were totally committed looked at your family as if it were sacred. That kind of veneration was not shared by the adults who acknowledged God only on Sundays and worshipped whatever they wanted on Monday through Saturday and it certainly wasn't there among the youth. You had to be careful who you trusted because the truth of the matter is that God's people can't trust anyone but Him. Only every now and again you could run into a human being with whom you could take that kind of risk.

Brie was one of those people. She didn't often know what to say when the problem was of a spiritual nature but she always listened. The Lofton/Paterson family wasn't big on God and going to church but they did believe some. Patricia never pushed her beliefs on Brie. She didn't want to push Brie away like that. Usually when she tried talking to friends about her belief in God, they'd disappear, so she stopped witnessing to others and that was why she was crying.

"What if Brie dies, China? What if she dies without having accepted Christ as her Lord and Savior? Maybe that was the reason for our friendship. If so, I have failed her and failed Jesus at the same time. Why was I so ashamed to talk about Him to her? I put my desires above her salvation. What if she dies, China? What if she goes to hell? Do you know whether or not she is saved?"

"I really don't know, Patricia. I don't know what to tell you," China said wondering about her own salvation and what it really meant. Was there really a devil and a hell? That was not a topic they discussed much. Actually, she never thought about it until now. She'd always run from the religious fanatics and Jesus freaks who approached her and when Rev. Boutier started preaching to them outside the pulpit, she tended to tune him out. She really believed that people who talked that "Jesus stuff" were crazy. Right now it seemed like something to think about. What if there was a hell and one of her best friends was on her way to it? "What do we do, Patricia? How do we help her? Is it too late?"

"My dad. Let's call my dad and ask him to come down here to pray for her. I am so scared. I'm not ready to lose her. Please God give her a second chance. Give me another chance to tell her about Your goodness, Lord. I won't fail You this time.

Please, God. Don't take her now," Patricia began to pray.

It seemed to be a bit much for China but she sat still as Patricia prayed aloud. Rather than being in agreement, China was more concerned about what the passersby would think. She bowed her head but she couldn't go as far as closing her eyes. She didn't want to appear to be strange.

As she vigilantly watched, from the knees down, those who approached the door, she noticed Brie's mother approaching. She raised her head to watch her. Something about her seemed different. As she neared the door, China realized that she was crying and did a double take before shaking Patricia to attention. "Mrs. Paterson?" she said in a barely audible tone.

"Is she crying?" Patricia asked. "Can't be. She's..."

She was interrupted by the abruptness of China's movements as she jumped up to run to Marlena's side. Before she knew it, Patricia was moving toward Marlena as well. The three women embraced before Marlena broke down and began sobbing in front of them. They helped her across the parking lot and into the emergency room.

Inside the emergency room, Ross was pacing the floor. He looked up and saw his wife who was being escorted toward him. He was surprised at Marlena's display of emotion and began to feel responsible for it. She reached for him and he opened his arms to accept her. "I'm sorry, Baby," he said. "I'm sorry to have been so rough with you but this was something that should have been more important than anything else you needed to do. That girl needs you more now than ever before."

Marlena sensed that "peacock-fanning-his-feathers" kind of pride in Ross. She didn't have the energy to burst his bubble and put him in his place by telling him that her tears had nothing to do with him. Her pride rose up but she chose to let him slide this time-- knowing that she would deal with his outburst later.

They hugged tightly but Marlena felt herself longing for Reggie. She needed Reggie's touch right now. She withdrew and began to sob leaving Ross dumbfounded. He didn't know what to do but felt a need to make her feel better. She walked away from him and sat in a chair near Nancy and Della. The two women walked toward her to comfort her and she accepted their affection. "How is she?" she asked them.

"We really don't know," Ross said. "She is still unconscious but they are working on her." Ross felt a distance from his wife that was familiar yet unusual. She was always distant but this was different. He usually attributed the distance to the fact that she took her work seriously but this wasn't the same. Perhaps the tears added a different twist but he wasn't sure that was it either. She didn't want to be touched by him. He felt like he'd violated her in some kind of way but wasn't sure what he'd done. Surely it couldn't have been the phone call and if that was the problem, so what. If she had been doing what any parent with half a decent mind would have been doing, i.e. waiting in the hospital for some news, the phone call wouldn't have had to happen.

Ross' thoughts surprised him. The surprise was that it felt so good to finally take a stand! Ross felt as if he had awakened from 10 years of hibernation. This was definitely something that he was going to have to hang on to. His family had been telling him for years that he needed to stand up to her for a change. The problem was that they weren't always nice when they said what they had to say and that pushed him closer to her and further away from them. One day he looked up and realized that he had been alienated from his family completely. It had been years since he'd spent quality time with his mother, who really didn't care for his "snotty wife". His mother just didn't understand. Marlena wasn't "stuck up", she was just professional, and she was more maternal than his mother had realized. She just didn't show it. The fact that his mother "only saw Marlena's weak points" destroyed her relationship with Ross. That, of course, is the way Ross saw it-- until now. Now, it seemed, the animal in him had been unleashed and it had no desire to be tied up ever again. Ross actually felt free. It was time for him to take control of his life again. He was amazed at his lack of desire to find out what was eating at his wife. Although she was crying, he knew the tears were not for her daughter. He knew her well enough to know that there was something else going on. She just didn't seem to be as concerned about Abrie's condition as she should have been. Or was Ross being too callous?

"It's getting late and you ladies probably have other commitments. You don't have to stay if you don't want to. Ross and I will keep you posted on Brie's status. In fact, why don't you all go on home and come back tomorrow," Marlena said as she stood up to address all of the women. They all simultaneously looked at Ross for a response. He waved and nodded his head, letting them know that he agreed with his wife.

"Okay," said Della. "But we'll be back to relieve you in the morning so you can get some..."

"That won't be necessary. We can handle it from here," Marlena said, cutting her off and taking an authoritative stand.

"That will be fine," Ross said firmly. "Why don't we work out some shifts right now? I know that you all love Brie and when she wakes up, she will want to see as many of us as possible. In fact, we're not going anywhere so if you want to page me before you come up or if you want to check on her that would be fine. Here's the number," he said as he handed each of them a business card. "Thanks for being such wonderful friends," he said as he hugged each of them individually and walked them out to their cars.

"And what exactly was that about," Marlena snapped upon his return.

"It's about you always thinking you're at work. It's about you always feeling as if we are all your subordinates. We don't work for you. We are not beneath you and quite frankly, we are all sick and tired of being treated as if we are peasants fortunate enough to be graced by your presence whenever you do decide to come home from work!"

"I don't have to take this from you," she threatened.

"That's funny. I remember my mother using those same words in reference to my relationship with you. I wish I had listened. I've had enough, Marlena. You acted as though Brie were one of the Jane Doe's on a slab in the morgue. Do you always have to be the professional? Always?"

"Ross Paterson. This is neither the time nor the place for you to be restoring your manhood!"

"Spoken by a true ice princess. You said it. 'Restoring my manhood'. My mother, who I haven't spoken to in the last three years, told me that you were trying to take my manhood. I guess she was right, and you said it out of your own mouth..."

"Just what I need. First my daughter has a car accident, then my husband decides to be 'the man' and now I'm being compared to the old battle ax!"

"At times like this, I wish I had listened to that old 'battle ax'. If I had, all of my needs would be taken care of in an up-to-date fashion."

"What's that supposed to mean?" Marlena asked with a lump in her throat.

"I think this conversation is over. This is not the time or the place for us to be discussing this, but it does need to be addressed, and it *will* be in due time."

The truth of the matter was that Marlena knew exactly what he was talking about.

She hadn't prepared a home cooked meal in months. She was not taking care of his sexual needs and, for that matter, rarely even gave him good conversation. She knew that she hadn't been the kind of wife to him that she'd been to Reggie. Reggie would have never tolerated it but Ross did. He let her get away with too much for too long. He never insisted so she never did more than she felt like doing. He had always compensated. In fact, he overcompensated and truth be known, it got on her nerves. He seemed spineless to her. He wasn't like Reggie. Reggie was the perfect husband. He was the kind of man every woman wanted and needed.

Marlena began to really mourn for Reggie now. Tears began streaming down her face. She didn't want Ross to see her crying but Marlena was no dummy. She knew what her problem was. She wanted to love Ross but not as much as she loved Reggie. She didn't want to go through the pain and agony of losing Ross the way she did after Reggie's death. Loving was hard but letting go was the most painful thing she'd ever had to deal with in her life. Ross was a good man and had put up with more than he should have for years. She often wondered why he stayed with her.

Ross was really surprised at the argument he'd just had with his wife. He didn't usually argue with her. He usually gave her whatever she wanted but tonight was different. He couldn't handle the apathy and lack of concern she showed for Brie. Ross didn't have children of his own. For some unknown reason, he couldn't produce children and it was painful for him because he loved them so much. When he met his wife and her three, he realized that being a dad didn't mean that you had to actually sire the children. There were many children out there with absentee or deceased fathers who needed male figures in their lives. God was good enough to him to bless him with three very well-behaved ones. He had detected Marlena's apathetic behavior before and attributed it to the abrupt loss of her late husband but never, ever discussed it with her. He loved her and her children but he also felt sorry for them. He figured they'd be a perfect match; they needed him and he needed them. What Ross had never shared with his wife was that he'd lost his first love to breast cancer almost two years prior to meeting her. It was slow and painful. He watched her die and never believed that she had to die so soon. She didn't want to "go under the knife" because she wanted "to die with her body looking the way God made it". Ross watched the girl of his dreams suffer, knowing all along that a mastectomy could have saved her life. So Marlena wasn't the only one who had lost a loved one to a senseless death. It was just that she had always been so preoccupied with her loss and caught up in her own pity that she'd never reached out to him so he kept his loss to himself. Suddenly, Ross began to feel angry. He began to feel his own personal loss. The stress of everything that had taken place over the last few hours had begun to take its toll. Unbeknownst to Ross, his emotional dam had broken and for the next few months, the floodwaters would flow beyond anyone's control, especially his own.

SEVEN

WHEN PATRICIA WALKED IN THE door, her father, the well-known Reverend Jacob Boutier, was not pleased. Even though she was of age, she still resided under his roof and as far as he was concerned, she had to abide by his rules. Already, she had lied about where she was going to be. She had told him that she would be staying with Della to work on a project that was going to take all night long to complete. That was almost believable to him since she and Della worked for the same company, in the same job but at two different offices. Often they worked on proposals together and many times they'd ask for his opinion regarding the finished product. He was not ignorant to the fact that they were really seeking his approval and, fortunately for them, he was a real man of God who didn't thrive off the power that they were inadvertently giving to him. Della was like a daughter to him and he didn't mind her treating him as though he were her dad.

"I realize that you are a grown woman but..."he started when he heard the door close behind his easy chair.

"As long as you're living under my roof...," Patricia said with him in a tone that startled the two of them.

He stood up from his chair and turned to look at her. He saw a look on his baby's face that he had never seen before and his reaction to what he saw led her to burst into tears. The look on his face upon seeing her let her know that he was still "Daddy" no matter how old she was or what she said, and he'd be there to make it all better. Without realizing it, he had extended his arms and started toward her. She ran into his arms and as they embraced, the two of them fell over onto the couch.

"Daddy, Brie had a car accident and is in a coma. I just left the hospital. She took route 95 and Daddy I am so scared for her!"

The outfit his daughter was wearing confirmed for him that she'd not been doing what she said she was going to be doing but that didn't matter to him right now. He had been young before and he knew what it was like. He had trained her up in the way she should go so he knew she wouldn't depart from it. He expected her to test the waters someday and he had been blessed thus far. "Thank You, Jesus", he said aloud but under his breath.

"What?" she asked.

"Oh, I was just thanking Jesus that it was not you," he said with a sigh of relief.

"Daddy! This is not the time to think about you or your blessings. Someone very near and dear to me has been seriously injured and her life is hanging in the balance. That's why this world is in the shape it's in. People only think about themselves and don't ever take the time to reach out to others. Daddy, people are perishing and we're not doing anything about it. You have to pray for her, Daddy. She needs prayer right now, Daddeee!"

Having been in the ministry for more than two decades, the Reverend Boutier could see right through this one. "Sweetheart, what's really going on?" he asked.

"You don't believe me? Do you think I made all of this up?"

"No. I don't think you made any of this up. It's just that I know you and I know how it is when you know Jesus but you don't think to share him with someone you care for until tragedy strikes. We can pray for her but we've got to take care of you first. Sweetie, God is not going to hear your prayer when you're not focused on Him. You see, your focus is fear and shame right now. You feel like you've not done something that you should have done. It seems to me that you feel like you hid Him from your friend, which makes you feel badly. The first thing you need to do is confess what's bothering you. You need to recognize it and confess it to Him. Are you ready to do that?"

With tears streaming down her face, she nodded her head affirmatively and said "Daddy, I never shared Him with her because I thought she would call me a 'Jesus freak' like everybody else and not want to be my friend. She helped me get through so much while we were in school. She always seemed to understand what I was going through..."

"But what made you think she wouldn't have understood about Him? Do you think it was the 'devil' in her that made her so understanding? Jesus said 'a house divided against itself will not stand'. That means that if Jesus was in you and she was able to help you to stand, He must have been in her, too. If not, the advice she gave you would have encouraged you to go in the opposite direction. Was the advice or support that she gave to you something that encouraged you to stay strong in what you believed or to change your Godly principles?"

"She always encouraged me to be who I am. She always accepted who I was. She never made fun of me because I was a 'preacher's kid'. She seemed to respect that."

"Did you ever try to encourage her to do things that went against the commandments of Jesus?" he asked. "And when you answer that one, be totally honest," he concluded.

"No. We tended to follow the rules and stay away from things that would get us into trouble."

"Well then, maybe you shared more of Jesus with her than you think."

"What?"

"Sharing Jesus doesn't always mean speaking about Him. You can share Him by modeling His behavior and when the person you're witnessing to is ready to go to the next level, the Holy Spirit will lead him there. Maybe she wasn't ready yet to receive Him on that next level and it sounds like *you* weren't ready, either.

You see, many well meaning people make the mistake of going out on the front lines before they suit up for battle, which is in the 'whole armor of God'. That's why they are not successful in their attempts to witness to others. They do it because they think they are supposed to, not because the Holy Spirit has led them to do so. Remember what He said to Jeremiah, 'you must go where *I* tell you to go and say what *I* tell you to say'. He also said to King Jehoshaphat in II Chronicles 20:15-17, 'the battle is not yours, but God's...you will *not* need to fight in this battle'. Although He was talking about a physical battle in that story, those words also apply to the spiritual battles that we are involved in everyday. So don't beat yourself up, Baby. It wasn't time for you to do that with her. Neither of you were ready then, but now that you know that, you have to go to God and find out what He wants you to do and to be prepared for that mission. Only He can make you ready. You can't do it yourself. It sounds to me like this accident may have been to help the two of you. It couldn't have happened unless God allowed it. It didn't happen behind His back and not everything that seems bad to our flesh is all bad. At least He spared her life. Perhaps He allowed this because He knew that it would bring her to Him."

"You know something, Dad? When I was younger, I used to hate to tell you about things that went on in my life because I knew I would have to listen to a sermon but right now, I'm glad that you have that knowledge to give. Thanks, Dad," she said as they embraced.

"I know you guys hated the sermons but your spirit took in more than you realized. Most people don't want to hear the sermons or speeches until they are faced with crises. It's a shame that folks don't want God until they are in a crunch. If they had Him before that, they'd avoid a lot of unnecessary pitfalls. Are you ready to pray now?"

"Yes, Daddy and thanks again," she said as he pulled back from her and gently took her hands into his.

"Gracious Heavenly Father..." her father began.

Back at the hospital, although Abrie was not out of the woods yet, her condition was stabilizing. Her parents had been in the waiting room all night. They took turns keeping watch, leaving one at a time to get something to eat. Emotions were flying high and dining together was not something they were ready to do. They had their own baggage to deal with. Too many secrets kept them from being able to hold and support each other like a loving couple should in a situation like this, but *loving* was the operative word. Did they really love each other or had they gotten married to avoid being alone? Was "love" present in this affectionless marriage? They had never had to think about it before and this accident was going to put this marriage to the test. It seemed that, unbeknownst to themselves or each other, there were two other parties involved in their marriage who were going to have to stand up and be counted. Marlena and Ross would have to face the fact that Reggie and Bianca had shared everything in their marriage, including and especially their bed.

Secretly, Ross mourned and longed for the late Bianca Noland and Marlena did the same for the late Reggie Lofton. When interrupted by the other for any reason, Marlena or Ross snapped at, insulted, hurt or angered the other, widening the wedge that was being driven between them. On the Intensive Care Unit, there wasn't much change in Brie's condition. She did seem to be stabilizing but she was not awake, which was where her loved ones wanted her to be. She was unaware of the dark secrets, the hidden pasts, the lustful desires, and secret passions that were unraveling in the world as she knew it. No one involved had any idea of the catalyst this accident would prove to be in exposing them for who they really were.

EIGHT

THE VIBRATING OF ROSS' PAGER woke him up. He had fallen asleep on the couch and lost track of time. He looked at his pager and saw that it was 9:15 a.m. Marlena was fast asleep on a couch across the room from him. Ross felt a sense of resentment for her that he had never felt before. He realized that in the last few hours he had felt many emotions that he had never before felt in regards to his wife. The irony of it all was that he liked what he felt. It seemed to be a relief of sorts!

The second vibration of the pager brought him out of the zone he had entered. He looked at the name and number on the screen. Della had called him a second time. He went to the phone booth outside of the hospital doors to call her. He needed to smell the morning air and this was an excuse to do so. He dialed the number on the screen and Della answered from her cell phone. She was en route to the hospital.

"Hello," she answered.

"Hi, Della. This is Ross. You paged me?"

"Oh, Good Morning, Mr. Paterson. I was on my way to the hospital and I was wondering if you needed anything this morning."

"That was awfully kind of you, and please call me Ross."

"Okay, Ross. Is there anything I can do for you this morning? Do you need me to pick up anything, make phone calls or run some errands for you? I know you haven't had the opportunity to do much and I know you have to go to work at some point."

"Della, that's incredibly kind of you but I don't need anything and any calls I need to make can wait. I can always go to the office later to take care of any of the other things that may need to be taken care of. That's one of the advantages to being your own boss, but I do need to call my secretary. She'll be worried about me," he said as he chuckled. "One thing about Bertha is that she mothers me and makes me feel like someone really cares," he said as he chuckled again.

"But Mr. Paterson, lots of people care about you. You are very well loved," Della said.

"Well thanks, Della. I've always sensed that if I'd had another daughter, it would have been you or someone just like you. You're sweet."

"I try to be. Are you sure you don't want me to call Bertha for you?" she asked.

"No, but Thanks. I'd better call her myself. If you call, she'll think I'm out doing something I shouldn't be doing. But thanks for reminding me."

"Any news on Brie?"

"No. Nothing yet."

"Well, if you need anything you have my number. I'm only a phone call away."

"Thanks, Sweetie. You will definitely hear from me if I need anything," he said before hanging up.

Della felt pretty good about the phone call. She'd always liked Ross, although she never cared much for his wife, who was too cold-hearted for her taste. This woman was like the Wicked Witch of the West as far as Della and Brie's other friends were concerned. None of them were shocked by her behavior. "The only shocking thing," Della said aloud, "was the fact that she showed up at the hospital at all!"

Ross felt kind of special after the two phone calls. Della started his day off by calling to see if he needed anything and Bertha acted like her whole week was going to be shattered if he wasn't going to be in the office on Monday. Bertha was very concerned and really seemed sincere in her sympathy. Ross wasn't used to feeling like people cared about him. His relationship with his wife had been lacking for years and the only other woman who he felt loved him hadn't spoken to him in a while, thanks to his wife. He missed his mother. She had shown Ross love from the very beginning. His mother always believed in him and she supported him in everything he did unless she felt it would prove detrimental to him. Even then, she stood behind him like he was taking his first few steps of life and she positioned herself to catch him if he fell backward or toppled over. Ross felt really bad about the separation from his mother. He missed her so much but "when a man marries, he has to put his wife above any other woman, including his mother". She had told him that time and time again. That was in part why he never married Bianca. He couldn't imagine putting anyone above the woman who loved him more than anyone else. Bianca loved him and she loved his mother. His mother loved her, too, and did everything in her power to get him to see that she was definitely the wife for him but Ross was too selfish and set in his ways to see it. He didn't have a real reason not to marry her but that he "wasn't ready". Needless to say, he never had the chance to "get ready".

"Ross, what are you doing out here?" he heard Marlena ask.

Ross looked at the time on his pager and realized that he'd been standing outside at least twenty minutes. Marlena had awakened about ten minutes after he did and didn't see him. That was a little disturbing to her. It was the first time in nearly ten years that she'd awakened with him away from her side. That left her with a funny taste in her mouth. For a second, to her, he seemed so far away.

"I needed a breath of fresh air," he mumbled as he returned to the waiting room leaving her outside.

"Ross," she called after him. The automatic doors shut behind him. Dumbfounded, she hesitated before going after him. "Ross, this is not the time to exert your newfound manhood. We need each other more than ever before."

"Lena, I needed you years ago and you were never there for me. I was always there for you and you made that so difficult for me. Right now, I don't need you at all. In fact, I don't even want you. After Brie gets better, I think I'm going to leave you because I just don't want to live like this anymore," he said, shocking not only her but himself, also.

"Ross," she gasped, "this is not the time or the place for this!"

"Oh, no? Now's as good a time as any as far as I'm concerned. What do you care? You have never cared about any of us. The only thing you ever cared about was Reggie Lofton and I am sick and tired of living in his shadow. I'm not Reggie and I don't want to be. Maybe you need to find yourself another ball of clay that you can mold into Mr. Reggie Lofton. Like my mother told me a long time ago, I don't deserve to be treated the way you treat me. I should have listened to her."

Marlena was totally unprepared for the things that came forth from her husband's mouth. She was absolutely shocked and had nothing to say. There was nothing she *could* say because he and his mother were right.

"Mr. and Mrs. Paterson," called out a doctor who was looking at a chart.

"Yes," they said in unison.

"There hasn't been much change in her condition, though it looks like she's going to pull through. Because we don't know the extent of the internal damage yet, it's hard to be any more specific about her prognosis. You might want to go home and get some rest. If there is any change, we'll contact you immediately."

"Do you have all of our information there? You know, like cell phone numbers and pagers and..."

"Yes, Sir. We have it all here."

"Please take care of my baby, Doctor," said Ross. "She's all I have."

"We'll do our very best, Sir."

At that, they both turned and walked away, leaving Marlena standing there.

"The least you can do is wait. You don't have a car here, remember?"

Ross didn't even look back and to her surprise, he caught a cab! She had been married to Ross Paterson for nearly 10 years and had never seen this side of him. She did not know the person who had been in the emergency waiting room with her.

Marlena shrugged her shoulders and began walking to her car, confident that he'd be at home waiting for her when she got there. She was tired of this little game and was going to give him a piece of her mind because of his childish behavior. She was going to straighten "Mr. Ross" out once and for all. She knew she should have handled him when he got out of line with her over the phone, and she was going home to make sure that he never, ever made that mistake with her again. Who the hell did he think he was? Before she knew it, her anger had her marching rather than walking to her car. When she reached her vehicle, she opened the door, put the key in the ignition, started the car, slammed the door, put the car in reverse, backed up, popped it back in drive and sped off. She couldn't wait to get home. The more she thought about his behavior, the angrier she became.

"Where to?" the cab driver asked.

"Huh?" Ross stumbled.

"I love you too, Sweetie, but you can't stay here. You've got to go somewhere," the driver joked.

"Oh, sorry. Uh," he hesitated, "4549 Oak Tree Drive. Yeah, 4549 Oak Tree Drive."

"You sure?"

"Positive. I've been needing to do this a long time so step on it," Ross asserted.

"Man, you've been watching way too many movies. What do you think this is? D.C. Cab? Do I look like Mr. T. or somebody? You gonna pay the ticket, Mr. 'Speed Demon'?"

"Alright already, man. You've made your point," Ross said, putting an end to the badgering.

It took about twenty minutes but they finally made it to his destination. Ross got out of the car, paid the cabdriver and stood in front of the house for a few minutes as the cabbie drove off.

"Home," he said, "it's so good to be home." He started walking and ended up in a skip as he reached the door.

NINE

THE CLOCK ON THE NIGHTSTAND showed four big numbers that led China to decide to get out of bed: 10:15. She'd slept away half the morning, which was okay since it was Saturday anyway. She attempted to sit up but couldn't. She was so exhausted.

She grabbed at her temples as if to stop the throbbing of the headache that had kept her up for a couple of hours after she'd gotten home. Her alarm had gone off exactly three hours earlier, which didn't help her in her current state.

"Another migraine," she said aloud but as softly as she could. "These things are coming more and more frequently. Perhaps I should go and get this checked out."

"Mom," a sweet little five year old voice seemingly screamed.

"Not now, Angie. Mom has a headache," she said as her daughter jumped on her bed.

"Please, baby, don't do that."

"But Mommy, I want some pancakes. I'm hungry," she said.

"Don't even try it, Little One. You've been fed this morning. Now come on out of here," said Damitria as if on cue. China's only sister lived with her and kept her daughter for her whenever she needed a sitter. Damitria was told a few years before that she couldn't have any more children, so it was a real delight for her to keep Angie for China. Daniel, her six year old, was in another room watching cartoons.

Judging by the look on China's face, Damitria sympathetically asked "another migraine?"

"How did you know?"

"Sis, you really need to get that checked out. It's beginning to scare me."

"I think you've been around me too long. You're starting to echo my sentiments."

"So does that mean that you are going to have it checked out?"

"Looks that way. Did I tell you that Abrie had a car accident last night?"

"You're kidding," Damitria gasped. "Is she alright?"

Grimacing from the pain, China answered, "no. She's in a coma. That's where I was all night. She was on her way to meet us at the new club in Ravenwood but she didn't make it. She took route 95 and somehow lost control of her car."

"Oh, Sis. That's terrible!"

"Yeah. After being around hospitals and sudden tragedy, you start to think about your own mortality. I think I'd better get my head checked out. Life is so fragile. It can be gone in a minute and you never know when your number's coming up, you know? You're here today and gone tomorrow. I got a reality check last night. I have to honestly say that I'm not sure whether or not she's going to make it..."

"Oh, don't say that! She's going to make it. I know she will!"

"I don't know. I guess you had to be there..."

"But where is your faith? God can do anything. You know that He can do the impossible, so it doesn't matter what you saw. Whose report will you believe? You've got to have faith."

"You know, last night, Patricia started talking all of that God stuff, too."

"He's probably trying to tell you something and I sure hope you're listening!"

At that, Damitria laughed. China attempted to do so but her headache stopped her from doing too much of that.

"Well, I guess I'd better go and check on the rug rats. I'll be back to check on you in a little while. In the meantime, I'll keep the noise to a minimum and the blinds closed tightly."

"Thanks," China mumbled.

Damitria knew how to take care of her sister and for that, China was very grateful.

Damitria knew what to do because she had to do it often. She was very concerned about her sister's problem. The migraines were coming too frequently and they seemed to be getting worse and worse. She actually left the room because she felt the need to pray. Abrie needed prayer and so did China. Although they had gone to church many times as kids, they didn't learn much about who Jesus was. After Damitria's medical problems that resulted in her nearly missing the opportunity to be a mother, she learned that Jesus was not only a friend, but a comforter. She knew that His arms were bigger, warmer and wider open than anyone else's. After discovering her endometriosis, she went into a depression that her family and friends didn't understand. They didn't understand why she wanted a lot of children. One of her friends had the unmitigated gall to tell her that she now had a free ticket to have as much sex as she could because she didn't ever have to worry about getting caught! That is life, though. Those who have the ability to have children don't understand it as the gift it is. Those who are barren know exactly how precious the gift of having children is.

"Hey, you two," Damitria said as she entered the room where the children were.

"Is my mommy going to be okay?" Angie asked.

"Sure she is," Damitria answered. "Why would you ask that?"

"I don't know. The angel said that it is time for her to go home," Angie said. "He said that everything was going to be okay, though. But we really need to pray for her. Auntie Dee, can we pray for her now?" she asked as she climbed down from her chair and got on her knees and into praying position.

"Sure, Baby Girl," Damitria found herself saying. She wanted to ask questions but couldn't because she felt a strong urging to pray for her sister, too. That urging was in part due to the fact that she had sensed the same thing. She sensed that her sister was going to die. The kids began to pray for China with Damitria leading the prayer. Damitria spent a lot of time talking to the children about Jesus and who He was. They believed in Him and their belief was unadulterated. It was easier to talk to the kids because they weren't afraid to believe. They were not afraid of other people thinking they were strange for believing in the most powerful being in existence. He wasn't a fairytale character to them. Nor was he a genie who granted them their wishes. He was real to them and the children helped her to believe in Him. They encouraged her when she had doubt. They touched and agreed with her when she needed a boost of faith, and right now was one of those times. She knew in her heart that her sister was going to die and that she would have to take on the responsibility of raising her niece as her own. It would be a bittersweet event, but she knew it was going to be okay.

TEN

Nancy had awakened around 10:30 a.m. and immediately began pacing the floor. She was mulling over the events that had taken place over the previous 12 hours. The five women had known each other for the last few years and their bond was getting stronger by the year. Immediately becoming more like sisters than friends, their relationship solidified while at the university together. Though they were not all the same age, they had heard of each other due to their high schools being in the same athletic league. All of them were involved in sports, band or other extracurricular activities at their high schools but ended up attending the same university and living in the same dorm. They began spending time together and carpooling home on holidays and weekends. Nancy was the most responsible of the group and very quickly took on a leadership role. Patricia was the most sheltered and also the baby of the bunch. She was by far the most naive. Della was the fantasizer. She thought the world was ideal and somehow reality often seemed to escape her. She married right out of school and needless to say, it didn't last very long. China was the wild one of the bunch and really was more of a bad influence than anyone else. She believed you only live once and should have as much "fun" as possible. She was fun, funny and always good for a laugh, whether it was ethical and moral or not. She had more man trouble than any of the others because she placed too much value on having one in her life. He didn't have to be a man; just male. Personality and qualities didn't matter. Ethics and values didn't matter to her either. The only prerequisite to being her man was that he was "born" male.

Finally there was Abrie who was, by far, the most well rounded of the entire group. She never judged the others and she always understood what they were going through. She was also the prettiest, which was a hard call because all of them were very attractive. The barometer was the number of men who would gravitate toward her before any of the others. It always seemed that she had the pick of the litter and always "caught" first. It seemed that the other women would only be asked out if Abrie was not there or already had a date. The beauty of it was that if you didn't notice her beauty, it would go without mention. Abrie never discussed it and never gave any energy to it even when someone else would bring it up. It just wasn't her thing. She carried herself very well and cared for her looks, but it was clearly not an issue for her.

When Nancy finally sat down, it was 11:00 a.m. She had been pacing the floor and thinking about her friends for thirty minutes. Nancy was also a worrier. She was too serious about everything and often criticized the others for not taking life seriously enough. They never took it personally and that sometimes offended her. Once she was accused by China of being a "Marlena Paterson wannabe". That made her cringe. If she had a role model anywhere, it would not be Mrs. Marlena Paterson! She remembered having met Abrie's mom and wondered how in the world such a "Medusa" could raise such a fabulous daughter; but then she met Ross. And that's when it began. For years she had written it off as a silly crush on her friend's dad but last night, things had gotten stirred up again. It seemed that when she saw how he was treated by his wife, she wanted to jump in and give him what he deserved. In her heart, she knew that there could never be anything between them but she didn't see the harm in having an affair of the heart; but that was before things spun out of control.

Though Nancy dated a lot, she had trouble finding men who could hold her interest for long. She found most men incredibly boring. For a minute, she thought there was something *wrong* with her but she realized quickly that she was not one who could date on the same side of the fence. That was a welcomed relief! She figured the problem to be age and immaturity. She found that she really had nothing in common with men her age. She discovered this five years ago when she met Ross Paterson. There was an instant attraction on both parts when they met. He clearly found her attractive intellectually and in appearance. She could feel the chemistry and so could he and if you know anything about that kind of chemistry, you know that it is *never* one-sided. They talked quite a bit when they first met but after a couple of visits, he started limiting their conversations and avoiding any contact with her for extended periods of time. She understood but didn't like it. She was very attracted to Ross and seeing the kind of treatment he got from his wife didn't help her in her quest to stay away from him. She found herself empathizing and sympathizing with him and that was drawing her closer to him. He was a sensitive man and his vulnerability was obvious. He needed to be loved and appreciated, and the nurturing side of Nancy drew her straight to him. Once, at a party, Marlena had been extremely rude to him in front of others. Shortly after that, he retreated to a back room. On her way to the bathroom, Nancy ran into him--literally. As they turned around and faced each other, there was a magnetism that drew them together in a nearly passionate kiss but fortunately, Ross had incredible self-control. The closeness of their bodies let her know, without a shadow of a doubt, that he was interested in spending time with her intimately but he pulled away from her and walked swiftly in the opposite direction. They never spoke about that incident--at least not verbally. They would exchange glances that spoke a thousand words but Ross would never act upon his desires. Many times Nancy would feel offended and rejected but there was nothing she could do. Ross was not the kind of man to cheat on his wife, regardless of the situation. That, in itself, was attractive to Nancy. His self-control was unlike anything she'd seen. Though he never said it in words, he communicated well that he was not that kind of man. A younger man, and many older ones for that matter, would have jumped at the chance to have

Nancy. She was, after all, beautiful, intelligent and very classy.

Last night, Nancy knew that Ross was vulnerable. That was one of the reasons she went to the house to tell them of the news. She wanted to be there for Ross because she knew "the ice princess" wouldn't. She knew he needed to be held and that there would be no female arms to do that for him; not with Abrie in the hospital. Abrie loved her dad and he loved her. It was a good, clean, healthy kind of love. She wasn't compensating for her mother. That was not the kind of love they had for each other. In fact, Nancy envied that, too. Her relationship with her father was very strained but not because of him; it was because of Nancy.

Nancy, like Patricia, was a preacher's kid whose dad followed the Bible as best he knew it. He took his family to church on Sundays and lived a very clean life until Sophie. Sophie joined her father's church a few years before he accepted the assignment in Pennsylvania. They were originally from New York and so was Sophie. What Nancy didn't understand was that part of the reason her family moved was because of Sophie's obsession.

Her father was a very quiet man who didn't air his dirty laundry in public. When Sophie started pouring it on thickly, her father never mentioned it. He handled his business by himself. He didn't want to disturb his family and he didn't want to upset the woman he'd loved for so many years. He thought the world of Nancy's mother and would never do anything to hurt her. One evening after service, Nancy was sent to the Pastor's Study by her mom to deliver a message.

Not knowing that Sophie was in there, she burst in the door in time to see Sophie back her father into a wall. Nancy, being young, didn't understand what she'd seen. She just assumed her father was being unfaithful. Unbeknownst to her, she had gotten her father out of a tight spot. Her father was not the cheating kind, but he was not much of a talker outside of the pulpit. He never mentioned what had happened and neither did she, but she *did* hold it against him for years. What she didn't realize was that her major attraction to Ross was that he was so much like her father! He was a very loving, loyal man who did everything to keep peace in spite of any extenuating circumstances. She hadn't realized that about him until now!

"Oh, my God," she exclaimed. "All of this time I thought Daddy was up to no good. My dad was resisting her. She was in his face and had him hemmed up against that wall. It wasn't him. It was her!" She began pacing the floor again. Pacing was a bad habit she had, which she had picked up from her father. The truth was that she was very much like him. The problem was that she'd seen him as a perfect being until she saw him commit an imperfection for which she'd never forgiven him. Everyone knew that Sophie was obsessed with her father, including her mother who wasn't worried about it in the least. She knew her husband was a true man of God and that his heart belonged to her. She also knew, being the first lady of a church, that there would be many scandalous women lurking around the pulpit. It was one of the devil's oldest tricks; if he could tear down the first family he could surely get the rest of the church. Fortunately, her dad's first love was Jesus. He

was very, very committed to his ministry-so much so that he moved his family rather than running the risk of tearing down the church. The way he saw it, he wasn't going to let Satan ravage his church. He'd known for a while that it was time for him to go elsewhere and that God had changed his assignment for a reason. Sophie was just sent to make him answer the call. God allowed it because He knew that Nancy's father wouldn't fall for it and that it would be enough to make him want to move from that particular church. When a person is loyal, it takes an act of God to get him to cut or sever his ties.

Prior to that incident, Nancy and her father had been very, very close. Her dad had sensed the distance but never bothered her about it. He just prayed. He knew that he had favor with God and that his baby would be okay. He also knew that he couldn't fix this and that he had to truly rely on God to work it out. Sometimes things take time because God sees the bigger picture. God knew that Nancy would have to go through this to be prepared for other things He had in store for her. Not judging a book by its cover was one of those things. She also learned that unforgiveness could and would prove to be very, very destructive and because of these two things, she'd lost precious time with the man she loved above all others.

ELEVEN

WHEN ROSS GOT TO THE door, he found it open and he let himself in. His mother was surprised and so were his father and two brothers who were there visiting their parents.

Ross was not surprised to see them there because it was customary for the Paterson family to have breakfast as a family on Saturdays.

"Sweet Jesus," his mother cried. "Son, is that you? Thank you, Lord God Almighty."

"Hello, Mom, Dad, Amos and Freddie."

"Lord, I knew You would bring my baby home," his mother shrieked as she ran over to grab him and hold him in her arms. Everyone else spoke back, shook his hand, hugged or high-fived him. The welcome was very warm and the atmosphere was as if nothing had ever been different. It certainly didn't feel like a homecoming. It was more like he'd never left and they had set his place at the table because they were expecting him. His mother got up and fixed him a plate of food. The boys had been talking sports, shop and God. The sports and shop was easy talk for him but talking about God was a little awkward because Marlena was not into Him. She didn't talk about Him nor did she want to hear about Him. She hadn't always been that way though. From what Ross understood, she became that way after Reggie died. Before that, the Loftons went to church as a family. After that, Ross would take his stepchildren to church but Marlena rarely, if ever, went with them. If she did go, it was to placate him; not because she wanted to.

"Man, what's wrong with you?" Freddie asked.

"Huh-what?" stumbled Ross.

"Dad asked you a question. Did you even hear it?" Freddie laughed.

"No, I didn't, Pops. I'm sorry. What did you say?" Ross apologized.

"How's the wife and kids?" his father asked.

"They're okay," he said.

"So what brings you over this way?" asked Amos.

"I've been doing some reflection and I realized that I hadn't seen you in a while so I came over. Is that, alright, Big Brother?"

Everyone laughed and hugged some more.

"It has been a while but thank God you're home. It's so good to see you, son," his mother said as she smiled and grabbed him around his neck. They fellowshipped as a family until Amos got up to go home. He said he'd had some errands to run and wanted to go and relax as he worked on a hobby in his yard. Before leaving, he asked if Ross wanted to go. Ross jumped at the chance to be alone with his brother so that he could tell him what was really going on. As Ross rose up from the chair to go to the door, he noticed a picture of Bianca on the mantel. He tried not to draw anyone else's attention to what he was doing so he moved slowly toward it, doing everything he could to remain inconspicuous. As he moved closer, he noticed a couple of other pictures that he had taken with Bianca laying flat on the mantel. He realized then how much his parents had loved her.

Bianca was beautiful. Her smile was an award-winning one as she had been crowned "Miss Pennsylvania" in her younger years. She was well liked by many but had her share of "haters" around her. Ross remembered a specific incident where a woman who had called herself "Bianca's friend" contacted him by phone to tell him of the "wretched woman" he was involved with. She told him that she was concerned about him and wanted him to know what he was dealing with. She proceeded to tell him about her sordid past and that she had seen Bianca pulling up into her ex boyfriend's garage just before she dialed his number. Well, Bianca was sitting right next to Ross when the phone call came in. Ross remembered having told the caller to "hold on", handing the phone to Bianca and saying, "Babe, it's for you!" Upon hearing Bianca's voice, the caller hung up. He never told Bianca who it was. He figured what she didn't know wouldn't hurt her, and it didn't.

"Let's go Little Brother," Amos said as he opened the door and walked out. Ross said his goodbyes and went out after his brother.

"Where's your car?" Amos asked.

"I caught a cab."

"From Where?"

Ross explained to his brother all that had happened over the preceding eighteen hours. His brother understood, as Ross knew he would. He told his brother about his changing feelings and that he hadn't mourned Bianca's death like he should have. His eyes welled up with tears but he didn't cry. His brother proceeded to tell him that everyone in the family understood and had been praying for him. They kept him in prayer because they knew that he was hurting and sympathized with him. No one took his distance personally. He went on to explain that times had been rough for their mother because mothers are concerned about everything and they get pretty emotional, but the boys in the family understood.

Though Ross appreciated his brother's support, he resented him having brought up Marlena. The anger he had for her had not yet settled. He didn't want to discuss her so he didn't, and Amos didn't ask again. He got the hint the first time and figured that when his brother wanted to talk about his wife, he would. By the time they reached his brother's house, the subject had been changed. They went to work on an old engine that his brother was rebuilding. He was a mechanic by trade and enjoyed his work to the fullest. Ross was a very successful contractor with some experience as a mechanic on the side. Their father was a successful mechanic, so it was in their genes. They laughed and talked about old times, watched a couple of movies and played some card games. As the sun began to set, Amos became a little concerned.

"Ross, I know that this is none of my business, but shouldn't you at least call the hospital to see if there has been any change in Abrie's condition?"

"I called earlier while you were outside. There's been no change."

"Okay. I won't ask any more questions," Amos said.

"Good. Now put in another movie," Ross demanded jokingly. And Amos did just that. Amos' wife and daughters were vacationing in New York at her mother's house. They had just left and weren't due back for another two weeks. Amos appreciated the company.

TWELVE

Marlena got home and stormed into the house. She called out to Ross, telling him that they had to talk. After not getting an immediate response, she scolded him for ignoring her. After a couple of minutes, it dawned on her that Ross *may not* be there so she began storming through the house. She first checked all of his favorite places inside the house and then the backyard. She was stunned to find that he was *not* there! Rather than thinking that he may have gone somewhere else, she assured herself that he'd be walking through the door any minute. She decided to wait for him in his favorite easy chair. The drumming of her fingers on the arm of the chair signified her impatience with the situation and her increasing anger. When she woke up nearly two and a half hours later, he was still not there. She began to feel a little uneasy but her pride wouldn't let her admit that she cared. She grabbed the remote and turned on the television set to find some news but after flipping through the channels for several minutes, she flung the remote across the room, stood up from the chair and began to pace the floor. Trying to find something to do to change the course of her thoughts and the impending events of the day, she called her office to find out if anything of interest was going on there. Finally, she decided to go back to the hospital where she discovered that Abrie's condition had not changed. Her daughter's life hung in the balance and her husband was nowhere to be found. Marlena decided to make a day of it in the hospital with her daughter. While sitting in a bedside chair staring at her daughter's nearly motionless body, she thought she'd seen her eyes open. Standing up abruptly to get a better view and seeing no supporting evidence of the movement, reality finally set in. It dawned on Marlena that her daughter may not recover from the accident. The revelation hit her so strongly that she nearly passed out. Her body swayed for a couple of seconds and she luckily caught herself before dropping to the floor. Suddenly, she'd lunged toward Abrie's body with outstretched hands like a young mother trying to catch her infant from rolling off the bed. "Brie-Brie," she cried. "My baby. What is happening here? Baby, hold on. It's going to be all right." A nurse who had been standing nearby offered her some physical and emotional support. A sobbing Marlena began to ask the nurse several questions regarding her daughter's condition but this time, the barrage of questions came from the heart of a mother. It was as if something inside her had snapped into its rightful place. Flashbacks of the "Jane Doe" in the morgue flooded Marlena's mind. She remembered the dizziness and the vomiting she'd experienced before leaving the office and finding out that her own daughter had been in an accident. Marlena began to feel overwhelmed and it must have shown on her face because the nurse asked her if they could give her anything. Before she knew it, three more nurses had entered the room. That was all she remembered before everything went black.

Della, who had reached the hospital shortly after Ross and Marlena had left earlier that morning, was two floors down in the hospital cafeteria reading the newspaper. She pushed back the cup of "mud" that she had been sold when she'd asked for a cup of coffee. "Must have been last week's brew," she mumbled to herself. "I guess I'll go to the nurse's station to see if there's been any change," she said as she started toward the elevator. The elevator doors opened to let someone off and Della picked up her step to catch it before the doors closed again. There wasn't much space left in the crowded elevator and the stare of the medical assistant who was standing at her side made her feel like there was even less space than there really was. He kept looking at her and was obviously not aware of the fact that his mouth was wide open. She thought to turn to him and say something like, "you can close your mouth now" or "take a picture; it will last longer". The thought of the latter statement being so very juvenile nearly caused her to choke on her laughter. Fortunately, his stop was the next floor. He and about three other people got off and the doors shut in his face as he turned around to take a last look. As the doors shut, she got a good look at him and almost wanted to stop the elevator to get off with him. He was absolutely gorgeous. He had silky smooth skin and the goatee around his mouth was as neat as a pin. The eyes that had been staring at her were very soft and caring. "Shoot," she said under her breath. "Oh, well. He was probably married anyway," she said as the doors opened to her floor. As she walked down the corridor, she saw a lot of activity near the doorway of Abrie's room. She briskly walked by the nurse's station unnoticed due to all of the commotion. She saw them putting Marlena on a gurney and gasped. "What happened here," she said in a louder than normal voice.

"Miss, you can't be back here," a male nurse said.

"I know this woman. She's my friend's mother. Has anyone notified her husband?"

"Miss, you can go to the nurse's station to give information if you have any but you can't be here," he said. "Please leave before I call security."

Della turned to go to the nurse's station when a hospital employee who wasn't quite as "rude" approached her to get some information from her. This person seemed to be genuinely interested in contacting someone for Marlena. Della offered to call Ross for them but the employee insisted that it was hospital policy for them to do the calling. At that, Della gave her Ross' business card.

In the middle of the third movie they watched, Ross' pager went off. He recognized the number of the hospital, jumped up, grabbed the phone and dialed the number without saying a word to his brother.

"Mr. Paterson, you need to get down here as soon as possible..."

"Has there been a change with Abrie? Please tell me it's not worse. What happ..."

"It's not your daughter, sir. There's been no change in her condition. It's your wife," the nurse interrupted.

"Oh, really," Ross exchanged. "What's wrong with her?" he asked dryly.

"We don't think it's serious. She collapsed, probably from exhaustion and the stress of it all. Nonetheless, she needs you..."

"She doesn't need me; she's got a whole hospital of people to take care of her. She'll be fine," Ross snapped. "Contact me if there has been some change in my daughter's condition before I get back there. I should be returning in the next couple of hours." At that, he hung up the phone and continued to watch his movie. He didn't even discuss it with his brother who was lying down on the couch opposite him in utter surprise. He couldn't believe the coldness in Ross' tone, but what was worse was that his brother's subsequent actions coincided with the apathy expressed over the phone.

Ross began laughing hysterically at the movie they were watching. The hysterics were not inappropriate, though; well, not exactly. They were appropriate because what he was laughing at was really very funny. They were watching an old "Smokey and the Bandit" but he just didn't seem moved by the fact that his wife and daughter were both in the hospital. He acted as if he'd just declined an offer from an old buddy who wanted him to come over and watch a taped version of a championship basketball game he'd already seen. Amos thought for a minute that this wasn't like Ross but he quickly remembered that it *was* just like him; the Ross that existed before Marlena. Had his brother returned to his old self? The family had been praying for that for years because they liked him the way he was. The Marlena influenced transformation was more than sickening. He was pure mush though he'd been raised to be strong, independent and self-sufficient. Over the years he'd turned into this pansy that couldn't make the decision to go to the bathroom by himself unless he'd asked Marlena, whose answer was more than likely going to be a resounding "no". The worst part of it was that the person the family once knew would *sit* there and hold his urine, rocking back and forth unless she told him to *stand* and rock! If you've never watched a family member go through that kind of change in the name of love, consider yourself lucky for it's not a pretty sight. On the other hand, if you have seen it, you know how gross it really is. It's absolutely disgusting.

Amos dared not question his brother about the phone call. He just lied in his spot on the couch pretending to be as interested in the movie as his brother. At that moment, he wondered why Ross had chosen to watch "Smokey and the Bandit". Quickly, it came back to him. Before Marlena, the family, including Bianca, would watch the reruns on television together. Bianca thought they were hilarious and whenever the family got together to do movie night, she would choose a movie from that series. Dad liked them as much as she did so there was never an argument or any kind of disapproval expressed by any other family member.

Was it possible that Ross was secretly beginning the grieving process? After all, he had mentioned earlier that he'd never really mourned her death as he should have. Could that be why he showed such a lack of interest in the fact that his wife was in the hospital or was he truly that angry with her? Who knew? Amos just knew not to ask; so he didn't.

Once the movie had finished, Ross asked Amos if he could drop him off at his house so that he could pick up his car. He said he had to get back to the hospital to check on his daughter but didn't want to "taxicab-it" back and forth and, "with the house being empty right now, this would be the best time to go and pick up a few things". Amos agreed to take him and drop him off but wondered what he was planning. What "few things" did he need to pick up and where was he going to go with them? It all seemed so strange yet Ross had plenty of reason to be in the place he was in. There were a lot of things on his mind that needed to be sorted out. He shrugged at it, deciding that if his brother wanted his help in the sorting process, he'd ask for it.

As he dropped Ross off, Ross asked that he keep his business under his hat. He didn't want the family to know anything just yet and expressed that once he'd cleared his mind, they'd be among the first to know. Amos agreed to keep silent and drove off.

THIRTEEN

"I'M AFRAID THERE'S BAD NEWS. Please, sit down. We found a malignant tumor about the size of a cantaloupe near the base of your brain and unfortunately, it's inoperable. I'm sorry. Who is the next of kin..."

"No! No, no, no!," China screamed and bolted straight up from the table. At the same time, Damitria came running into the examination room.

"Hey! Are you okay?" she asked as she noticed the ghastly look on her sister's face.

After taking a few seconds for her eyes to focus, China answered affirmatively.

Damitria embraced her sister gently and lovingly. She knew not to move too much or too suddenly due to the fact that her sister had been struggling with a migraine headache prior to falling asleep earlier. China rejected the embrace as she seemingly gasped for air. Damitria knew that something unusual had happened. China looked at Damitria for what seemed like ten minutes in a blank stare, as if she didn't recognize her. Damitria just stood still. Instantly she remembered what Angie had told her, and the reality of death set in. Wanting to cry, Damitria stared back at her sister, realizing that China also knew her fate. Neither of them said anything for a few minutes, each knowing that the other knew, too. Finally, China asked Damitria, "I'm going to die, aren't I?"

Looking at the floor and searching for the right thing to say, she mustered a "why would you ask me?"

"Because I know that you know."

"How am I supposed to know? I'm not a doctor..."

"You know. You know in your spirit," China replied surprising Damitria.

"What's that supposed to mean," Damitria asked.

"It's strange but for months I've heard you talk about the things that you felt in your spirit. At first I thought it was kind of odd and for a long, long time I thought you were crazy but you never let up so I just accepted it. It was too deep for me but you believed it so I didn't bother you about it. But now I know. I know that you feel these things in your spirit because somehow I feel it in mine and I feel in my spirit that you know that I am going to die."

Damitria's eyes welled up with tears. She did know but she was not going to answer that question for her sister. She just couldn't, so she stood there in silence.

"I'm going to make another appointment to find out what's really going on, but somehow I already know. I just know. It's like I have this peace on the inside of me that tells me that it's true. I know I'm going to die and so do you. I know you do so you don't have to say it."

After a few moments of silence, Damitria excused herself from the room and went into the waiting room to check on the children who had fallen asleep in front of a television set. She wanted to cry but couldn't. She knew that this was only the beginning and that she would have to be strong for all of them, including their mother and other family members. Who was going to tell them? Would it be her? She certainly hoped not, but if she had to, she knew she would.

FOURTEEN

ANOTHER DAY HAD PASSED AS Nancy contemplated calling her father. Even before the realization or revelation, which ever seems more appropriate, she'd often think about calling her dad. She missed him greatly but anger and pride kept her from doing what she'd known for a long time she needed to do. She picked up the phone several times that day but couldn't bring herself to call him, as her pride had very quickly turned to shame and embarrassment. She felt as if she couldn't face him and hung her head every time she thought about talking to him, as if she were no longer worthy of his love. She knew that he'd be loving and receptive of her phone call but it wasn't him that worried her the most. It was that she didn't know what to say, let alone how to start off the conversation. A lot of time had passed since she'd talked to him as a friend. She'd accused him for a long time of something he hadn't done and who would have thought that the way she'd find out his innocence would be through her own home wrecking, floozy-like actions? She had hated her dad because she thought he was doing exactly what she was trying to get Ross to do. She stopped speaking to her father for doing what *she* was doing--or trying to do. At no other point in her life had Nancy felt this low.

The ringing of the phone that jolted her out of the trance she was in seemed much louder than usual. She ran toward the phone, hoping that it would be her dad.

"Hello."

"Hey. Where've you been?" asked Della from the other end.

With an audible sigh Nancy answered, "I've been at home all day long. I was just thinking about some things and needed some time to myself. Did you go to the hospital at all today?"

"Yeah. As a matter of fact, that's where I am now. They just admitted Marlena..."

"Marlena?"

"Yeah. She apparently collapsed due to all of the stress surrounding Abrie's condition. At least that's what they think at the nurse's station."

"Unbelievable. Is there any news on Abrie?"

"None. There's been no change that I know of and I've been here most of the day."

"What about China or Patricia? Have either of them been there today?"

"Not to my knowledge. I haven't seen or heard from either one of them yet. The whole ordeal has been pretty frightening and I guess each of us is handling it in our own little way. There's really not much any of us can do."

"Yea, except pray."

"Yea, right. What's that? When was the last time any of us did that? It's a shame that we wait until there's tragedy before we decide to call on God, huh? I know that I haven't done any praying in a long time and I'm almost too embarrassed to call on Him now. He may not want to hear from me."

"Well, they say He's like a father to us, huh? I guess any real father would want to hear from you any time you call and for whatever reason, wouldn't you say?"

"I guess so. I've never been a father before," Della said with a chuckle that got no
response from Nancy.

"I mean, if you had children, wouldn't you want to hear from them at any time? Would it really matter how much time had passed?"

"Good grief, Nance. If you want to pray to Him, pray already! Why ask me a bunch of questions? Personally, I don't think He'll reject you, but there's only one way to find out and, by the way, *you're* the preacher's kid. Don't you remember the story of the "prodigal son"?

"Yea, but do you believe that stuff? Do you think life really works that way?"

"Honestly, I used to think those stories were myths the old folks would use to get us to behave the way they wanted us to. I don't know. I'm not the resident bible scholar but I know who is. Why don't you ask your dad? He ought to know. I mean, he's only been preaching for about twenty years or so. I'm sure he'll have the answers to your questions, don't you think?" Della asked innocently.

After a brief period of silence Nancy answered, "Yea. I guess he would have the answers. As a matter of fact, I know he would. Well, I've got to go. Keep me posted on any changes in Brie's condition, okay?"

"Well, I'm about to leave the hospital and go home. They're waiting for Mr. Paterson to get here. I guess he's on his way. Poor guy. Now he's got two family members to worry about..."

"Yea, I guess. Well, I've got to go," Nancy interrupted and abruptly hung up before Della could say another word. Della found her behavior to be odd but attributed it to the stress of everything going on. Even she was stressing, but not only about Abrie's condition. There were things going on in her life as well. For some strange reason, Greg entered her mind, but she quickly dismissed the idea that she could be missing him. He was definitely much more trouble than he was worth. The funny thing about life is that tragedy can tempt you to forget the things that really matter while substituting them for those that don't matter at all. For instance, Della could forget about what Greg had done, chalking it up to the foolishness of a man and let bygones be bygones under the auspices that life is short, but the truth of the matter is that he violated their wedding vows by committing the only acceptable reason for divorce even under Mosaic Law. Yes, the effects of this tragedy would make *her* see it that way, but would it affect him in the same way? Probably not. It wouldn't because Abrie was not his friend. Even before the accident, he'd only talk to her because he knew that she would bring his messages back to Della. Would he see it as an opportunity to get what he wanted, which was really his place back inside his comfort zone? By now, he's had enough time to see that the grass is not greener on the other side and that with Della, he stood to gain more than he would alone or with the other woman. In light of what has happened, could he be callous enough to take advantage of the situation? Sure he could. He was callous enough to commit adultery, steal the money from their bank accounts and leave her high and dry to fend for herself. And what was his motive? Self-satisfaction. Greg wanted what Greg wanted and that was all that mattered to him then and he's no different now. He's the same "selfish, egotistical bast..."

"Excuse me?" a voice asked as Della realized she'd spoken aloud. She looked up and the handsome medical assistant she'd seen earlier was standing behind her reaching for the phone. She looked down at her hand to see that she hadn't yet hung up the receiver.

Embarrassed and apologizing profusely, Della began to laugh hysterically. Abraham, whose name she found out later, was laughing along with her.

"An old boyfriend?" he asked.

"What?" she responded.

"The phone call. Was it an EX-boyfriend? At least I hope it was because if he weren't, he *would* be after calling him what you called him," he said and they both laughed some more.

"No. Actually, I was talking to a girlfriend of mine..."

"About an old boyfriend," he interrupted and they laughed again at his impeccable timing.

"Well, if you really want to know the truth, I was talking about an ex-husband of mine."

"How many ex-husbands do you have?"

"You're quite the funny one. You're pretty quick, too. What? Are you a comedian on your other job?" They both laughed.

"No. I'm really not. I am..."

"Just using this humor as a way to find out all of my personal business?"

"Well....yes. As a matter of fact I am," he said with continued laughter from the two of them.

"Well then, sir. The rest of the information is going to cost you dinner because I am starving."

"You took the words right out of my mouth. We can go to dinner under one condition."

"Uh-oh. Here it comes. And what might that condition be?"

"That we leave and not use the hospital cafeteria. I'm a little burned out on hospital food. I'm beginning to feel like one of the patients." At that he produced a small container of salt from his pocket that he carried with him to somewhat season his food on the nights he had to work late and couldn't go out for dinner. Fortunately for Della, this was not one of those nights. Before they left, she checked the nurse's station to find out if there'd been any change in Abrie's condition. She also checked in on Marlena, who was conscious but in a zone unfamiliar to her. There was an empty stare in Marlena's eyes that Della had never seen before but she knew better than to question it. Truth be known, the real reason she didn't ask was because she wasn't interested. Not only because she had a dinner date with a handsome and humorous man, but because Marlena Paterson was not someone she truly cared about. Maybe she needed this to humble her. In fact, in Della's mind, Marlena needed to be alone. "Alone," she heard herself say aloud. In that instant, she realized that Ross was not with his wife and that she had been standing outside in the hallway where he would have had to pass in order to get to her room. He hadn't passed by her at all, which meant that he wasn't there at all. That wasn't like Ross. He was always there for her but maybe this time he'd finally come to his senses. But why now? This was the time when she truly needed him most. With Abrie in the hospital... "My bad. Marlena has never needed anybody," she mumbled under her breath as she was walking toward Abraham.

"Excuse me? Do you do this often?" he asked and they both laughed as they walked arm in arm down the corridor.

FIFTEEN

"MONDAY MORNING AND I FEEL like I just got paid,"
Ross exclaimed as he woke up.

He looked around the hotel room he'd stayed in the
night before and was glad that he'd secured it for five
nights instead of one. It afforded him the opportunity
to get some much deserved shut-eye. It felt like it had
been years since he'd actually rested during his sleep.
With Marlena lying next to him, or not lying next
to him like she should have been, he tended to sleep
with one eye open and the other closed. His sleep was
never restful because he was always concerned about
her whereabouts--or maybe her "why-abouts". Why
wasn't she in bed with him? Why was she sleeping in
the easy chair instead of in bed next to him? Why did
she sleep so far away from him when she *was* in bed?
Why won't she cuddle up with him and why does she
jerk away from him when he tries to hold her?

"Why, why, why? Why do I ask why? There's never
a valid answer and for too many, many years, I took that
from her. What was wrong with me? Here's a why

for you, Ross Old Boy: why did you throw away your manhood for someone who was obviously in love with someone else? This isn't news to you. You've always known that you were a 'Reggie Lofton understudy'. Wake up old boy; it's high time you wake up!" He actually laughed at himself in the mirror before turning on the water to take a much needed shower. Bertha wasn't expecting him in too early this morning. He had called her at home on Saturday evening just before he had taken an all night drive to let her know that he would need some reflection time. He drove all night on Saturday and went to the hospital early Sunday morning. He stayed at her bedside as much as they would let him during the day on Sunday. He had been given time to talk to Abrie about what was happening to him. Although he wasn't sure whether or not she could hear him, he told her about Bianca and how much he'd missed her. Somehow he felt she'd understand. Actually, he knew that she was the only one who would even care to understand. She was a great listener and seemed to really be interested in the lives of those she loved; not as a busy body, but as someone who genuinely cared about those around her--a trait she obviously did not inherit from her mother who was quite the contrary. The thought of Marlena messed up his groove so he had to get up and walk around for a while. During that time, he took the opportunity to call Abrie's brothers to let them know what was going on. Neither of them could make the trip to Pennsylvania for different reasons but it certainly wasn't because they didn't want to. Ross discouraged both of them from rearranging their schedules because there was nothing they could do. He promised to keep them informed of any change but felt confident that Abrie was going to pull through this. How he knew that was a mystery to him, but he knew; he just knew.

Ross wasn't the only one with the confidence that she'd pull through. Della had a certain peace about it herself. Upon seeing Abrie's face, a peace came over her as if Brie had somehow reached her from the place she was in to let Della know not to worry and to tell the others not to worry. It seemed that she was just resting and somehow you just got that message when you went in to see her. Della almost felt guilty for not being at the hospital for twenty-four hours each day, although she was there at least twelve. Though she had had an awesome time with Abraham on Saturday evening, she avoided him on Sunday. She didn't want to give him "too much too soon". She spent much of Sunday reflecting on the time they'd spent together. She remembered most of all, that he was a natural gentleman who did all the things a classy lady would expect him to do--naturally. There was no faking and shaking with this one. He opened doors, pulled out and pushed in chairs, communicated with service personnel on cue, without ever missing a beat. The best part of it all was that he didn't seem uncomfortable with any of it. He'd taken her to one of the finest restaurants Ravenwood had to offer, with the drive up and the drive back seeming way too short for Della's taste. She was very comfortable with him and he kept her laughing. Because he was off the next day, they had the time to watch the sun rise, which happened to be extremely beautiful on that particular morning. It was as if God

Himself had painted a backdrop especially for them as they ended their evening. In fact, those were Abraham's words exactly, which was no surprise to her because with a name like Abraham, you know that somebody in his family had to be a believer in God. Speaking of which, one of the reasons she didn't see him on Sunday was because he'd gone to church. He'd said that he was attending two services that day but didn't invite her to either. "That was odd," Della found herself saying aloud.

"Hey, Dell. It's me...No, that won't work. Hi, Della. I was just thinking about you...Nah, that's kind of corny. Yo, Della. What up, cuz?" Abraham laughed at himself as he tried to figure out an appropriate message to leave on Della's machine. He figured she'd be at the hospital sometime today so calling and leaving a message would be okay. He didn't want to see her because he didn't want to give her "too much too soon". He was off on Sundays and Mondays so he knew he wouldn't run into her at the hospital but it seemed like eons had passed since he'd last seen her. That was odd for him because he usually grew tired quickly of the women he dated. In all of his thirty years, he'd never met a woman who brought him the kind of peace Della did. They didn't seem to have much in common, though. She'd been married before but had no children. He'd never been married but had one child--and plenty of "baby mama drama" to go along with it. They'd both been to college and that's about all he knew about her. Their time spent together was much more fun than informational. They both figured that those things would come in time and believe you me, Della would find out about Driscelle soon enough.

Abraham looked around at all of the glass on his floor from Driscelle having thrown a brick through the bedroom window of his house the night before. On the brick was a note saying that he would soon "pay for all of the trouble" he'd caused her. Although she didn't leave a name, he knew it was her because she always did stupid stuff like that. He'd grown tired of calling the police who would do nothing about it because he couldn't "*prove*" it was her. Driscelle was smart enough to wear gloves which left no fingerprints. She also knew his schedule so she'd know to throw the bricks just before he'd leave to go to work or immediately after he got home. Because of the seclusion of his neighborhood, no one ever saw her do her dirt. He only felt sorry for four year old "Little Abe".

Abraham met Driscelle in an accounting class that he'd taken as an elective. She was not too pretty but wasn't bad on the eyes. She thought she was much prettier than she really was, but that didn't bother him too much. He had never intended to get that close to her, but she'd had different intentions from the beginning. He often wondered if "Little Abe" was really his but was too scared to find out. He didn't want to know what he already knew to be true. The truth would leave the little boy without a father, and as crazy as his mother was, one could truly understand why he needed one.

The two of them spent very little time together and that's what always made her act out. She demanded that they spend more time, but he tried to make it very clear to her that he wasn't looking for what she was looking for in a relationship. She pretended to be okay with that for a while , but when the home-cooked meals started coming in, and the gifts for special (and not-so-special) occasions started showing up at his job and on his doorstep, he knew there was going to be trouble. He tried his best to back away from her but the more he stayed away, the more she pushed herself upon him. In every nice way possible, he told her that there was no chance of an intimate relationship between the two of them. She'd pretend to accept that but the drama in her life kept getting deeper and deeper. Time after time, she'd "just need a shoulder to cry on" and of course, his was the obvious choice. Why he didn't stay away from her, he'll never know. He was kind-natured and really didn't want to hurt her. What he didn't realize was that she was intentionally sinking her claws into him and before he knew it, she was pregnant. Looking back on it, he could see that this vixen had decided what she'd wanted and would, under no circumstances, take "no" for an answer. Because he'd only planned to be distant friends from the beginning, he never looked into her sordid past or her dysfunctional upbringing. What was intended to be a casual friendship on his part turned out to be a typical situation involving a man who was raised to be a gentleman but got tangled up in the web of a gold digging opportunist who just wanted to run back to her family and friends to tell them of the "find" she'd made.

Abraham's mother, though extremely disappointed, understood and was very supportive. She'd raised her son to take care of his responsibilities and to think twice before making decisions, but understood that, as in most situations like this, the good guys don't ever see it coming. They don't see it because they don't realize that "devils" like this exist. When raising a child to be respectful, often they are sheltered from the evils of the world and those unfamiliar spirits often don't become familiar to them until it's too late. His mother would have never allowed him to date a girl like Driscelle, so he didn't understand her "kind" when he met her. He believed her sob stories, felt sorry for her, wanted to help, and in plain words, fell for the okie-doke. On the only night he ever became intimate with her, her best friend was "dying of some strange disease," and Driscelle "just needed to be held". Come to find out, there was no terminally ill best friend and no strange disease. When his mother asked why he didn't protect himself, he told her that he had but Driscelle claims that there was breakage, and that was how "Little Abe" happened. Of course she claims that he was the only one at the time, but we all know better than that.

The boy doesn't look like him but nonetheless, he does need a father, and Abraham is the only father that he knows. Even if "Little Abe" wasn't his, he wouldn't mind adopting the little boy because, somehow, he turned out to be a really sweet kid. When Driscelle found out that she couldn't trap him into marriage, the beast in her really came out. She almost got him but something in him wouldn't let him go through with the nuptials. They'd made arrangements at a wedding chapel, rented tuxedos, invited a few guests and the whole nine yards—well, maybe eight of them. On the morning of the wedding, Abraham became as sick as a dog. He threw up all morning long and couldn't get out of bed. He tried and he tried but he couldn't. He vomited so much that he ended up having to be hospitalized from dehydration. Extremely furious and unwilling to believe the truth,

Driscelle brought the drama to the hospital. She swore he'd faked the sickness so he wouldn't have to marry her. Of course she would think that way because that's something she would have done. She stayed by his bedside in her wedding gown, but not because she cared about him. It was because she wanted to grab a chaplain to marry them on the spot as soon as Abraham could muster up enough wind to say "I do".

Fortunately for him, his mother was right there. She became suspicious of this woman's urgency to have him marry her and, in her infinite wisdom, convinced him to wait. She actually encouraged him to wait until the birth of the baby because it seemed to her that a paternity test may have been necessary. Abraham's mother was not the messy type. She didn't mean Driscelle any harm but she needed to protect her own. With that "mother's intuition", she smelled a rat and she had to do what any conscientious mother would have done. Because of the possibility of it being his, she encouraged him to take care of the baby as well as the mother. As far as she was concerned, Abraham still needed to fully understand the responsibilities involved in caring for a family. She didn't excuse his mistake, she taught him to live with it.

Naturally, Driscelle hated his mother. She faulted his mother for him not marrying her. For a few months, his mother took the insults with a grain of salt. She actually felt sorry for Driscelle but after a while, mom got that dip in her hip, put some base in her voice and handled her the way she would have handled the situation if her own daughter was disrespectful to her. It seemed that Driscelle needed some real mothering because through all of this, her mother was nowhere to be found. Actually, she could have *easily* been found. It would have just been a matter of looking in one of the local bars or checking for her at her home. If not in the bar, she would have most likely been passed out in the living room of her trailer. But who went looking for her? She couldn't have helped much anyway, due to the many problems of her own she carried around.

The nicking of his face brought Abraham back into the physical realm. He'd been shaving and thinking about all of the things that had happened to him in the last five years; five that had proven to be the worst of his entire life. Fathering a child with a woman you don't love is a real man's worst nightmare. The saddest part of it is that there are boys doing it every day without a second thought. It's as if it is a game to them. And we wonder why the world is in the shape it's in. People are committing heinous, loveless acts against others with not enough empathy being shown by the general public. It's because children need to be planned or conceived out of love, not from irresponsibility or indiscriminate sex as Little Abe was. But Abraham had learned his lesson. He didn't know how receptive Della would be to his way of handling it, though. He liked her, but he didn't know how she would handle his vow of celibacy. He'd been celibate for the last four and a half years and was hoping that she wouldn't think him strange because of it. Neither did he want to succumb to the pressures of having sex and end up in the same or a similar situation again. He knew it couldn't be the same because Della wasn't like Driscelle. He *knew* that spirit now, and could sense it from ten miles away. He'd come in contact with several women like Driscelle during the last four years, which helped him greatly in keeping his vow, but he knew that Della wasn't one of them. He also knew that this would test his strength, but he didn't want that struggle, either.

SIXTEEN

Because of the nature of her complaints and the fact that an appointment had cancelled, China was able to get some testing scheduled for the end of the week with the promise that if anything opened up before then, she would be the first to get a call. This was one of those times when having a family doctor would have been beneficial. Using an HMO wasn't so bad but if they'd known her personally, she probably would have been seen that afternoon. Waiting until the end of the week was going to be difficult. What was she supposed to think about or do between now and then? Funeral arrangements? Maybe that wasn't a bad idea, she thought.

"Mommy, I want to give you a hug," Angie said as she threw her arms around China's legs, breaking up her thoughts.

"You do," China asked in a mommy-like voice. "Then come up here," China said as she picked Angie up and gave her a smack on the lips. "How about a kiss, too?"

"Mommy, are you going to die?" Angie asked in a very serious voice.

Shocked and at a loss for words, China asked, "Now why would you ask me that?"

"The angel said you were going to die but it would be okay. Are you going to be okay, Mommy?"

"What angel?" China inquired.

"The one who was in my dream last night. He's a very nice angel, Mommy. He's my friend."

"Well, what else did this angel tell you?"

"Nothing. He just said that it was time for you to go home and that you would be okay. He told me to say prayers for you and that everything would be fine and then he went away. I like him, Mommy. I feel good when he comes around."

"Well if he's telling you to say your prayers, he must be a good angel, huh?"

"Yep! He loves me and he loves you, too! Can I have some pancakes, Mommy?"

"Huh? What?" China asked as if she'd zoned out for a second or two.

"Pancakes, Mommy. Pancakes," Angie celebrated.

"Sure, you can have some pancakes," Damitria chimed in as she walked into the kitchen and headed toward the cabinet.

"I'm not gone, yet," China snapped. "I can make my child some pancakes."

Damitria looked at her in utter surprise. China did not relent, but opened the cabinet to get a mixing bowl, then proceeded to the cupboard to get the pancake mix. Damitria retreated without saying another word. She stood silently for a few seconds, and then turned from the kitchen to check on her son. Not ten minutes later, Damitria finds herself running to the kitchen at the smell of something burning terribly. She looked over and found China crouched down on the floor smashing her temples between her hands and gasping for air. Damitria grabbed the skillet off the fire and dropped it into the dishwater that had been prepared for the cleaning of the kitchen. She spun around, led Angie, whose back had been turned to her mother, out into the hallway, then turned back to help China into the bedroom. On the way there, they made a much needed stop at the bathroom. China had begun vomiting. Damitria went to call for an ambulance but China told her of the appointment she'd just made. Upon calling the recently dialed number back, the nurse gave her some instructions for care and told her to bring her sister to the emergency room right away. By the time Damitria returned to the bathroom, China had passed out. Damitria turned around immediately and called for an ambulance.

"Hello."

"Hi, Dad."

"Nancy, is that you?"

"Yes, Daddy. It's me."

"Well hello stranger. I haven't heard from you in a while. Here, let me get your mother..."

"Actually, Dad, I called to talk to you."

"Is everything okay? Do you need something? Are you alright?"

"Yes, Dad. Has it been that long? Can't a girl call just to talk to the number one man in her life without needing anything?

"Well, I guess you could. It's just that it's been a while since you and I have had a chance to really talk. I guess I'm always on my way out the door and usually you talk to your mother about whatever you need."

Nancy could tell that he was trying to make it easier for her, and that was so much like her wonderful dad. He was always trying to make life better for everybody else. Perhaps that had been her problem but now was not the time to beat herself down. They talked for a few awkward minutes before she finally asked to speak to her mom. She told her mother about Abrie's accident and how it had made her take a look at her own life and how she'd finally begun to realize that life was so precious. She confessed to her mother that she'd not spent enough time with her father and wanted to do more with him in the near future.

"Oh, Baby. He'd like that very much," her mother said.

"What do you suggest? A father-daughter outing? I don't even know what he likes to do."

"He does need a break. Even if it's to come down and visit you for only a few hours. The only problem is going to be trying to pull him from his congregation to do that. They never stop to think that *he's* human, too."

"Mama, what's the matter?"

"It's that darned deacon board again. They want so much and expect your father to play God in the process. They don't read or study God's Word for themselves, yet they want to perform these 'miracles in the name of Jesus' that keep getting everybody else in hot water. They keep making these financial commitments for the church to fulfill without first consulting your daddy—their pastor! Then they want to get angry with him when he follows protocol and takes the financial matters to the business meetings for approval. It's as if they want him to shove money under the carpet to them so that they can appear to be personal heroes for the poor and needy in the community. But you know, their 'poor and needy' always tend to be related to them or to someone they know! Now, you know your daddy is a professional man. He's not going to do anything he shouldn't do involving the business matters of the church. He says he's not worried about it, but I know he is. You know how he starts pacing the floor to the point where you think he's going to wear a hole in the carpet? Well, he's been pacing a lot lately. Every morning, he starts in the bedroom and ends up in the kitchen. He doesn't really talk about it until he gets angry. Then he blows like an erupting volcano."

"Yeah, Ma. I know that one well," Nancy said as she thought of herself. Nancy and her mother finished their conversation and agreed to talk again soon to work out some plans for the father-daughter get away and then hung up.

"The ambulance is on its way, China. Just hang in there. Oh, help her, Jesus. Please don't let her die now. Don't take her yet. Please, God, let her at least say some proper good-byes." Damitria prayed by her sister's side until the ambulance got there. Of course the site of them taking away her mother led Angie into hysterics. Damitria did what she could to calm Angie down while putting the children in the car and following the ambulance. From the hospital, she called her mother and told her everything that was going on.

Meanwhile, on another wing of the hospital, Patricia was sitting at Abrie's window praying and silently talking to her friend. Only immediate family could actually go into the room so the friends had to stand outside the door or wait in the lobby. Instantly, she felt a real strong connection to Abrie, realizing that she didn't want her friend to die. Death was not an option for Abrie Lofton; she was too good a person. At that moment, Patricia made a vow before God and to her friend that she would come to the hospital and pray for her every day until God brought her out of the coma and made her well again: "Please, God, please," she prayed. "Give us a second chance."

TWO MONTHS LATER

"There," Marlena said. "These will look real pretty in this window, don't you think?"

She looked over at Abrie who was staring quizzically at the flowers and at the woman she would later recognize as her mother. She had been out of the coma for a couple of weeks and was making real progress. She didn't recognize anyone and didn't have full use of her fine motor skills. Her gross motor skills also needed a lot of work, but she was coming along fairly well. Marlena was there to assist her in the afternoon feeding as she and Ross took turns at mealtimes. He had been there earlier to do breakfast and Abrie seemed to respond to him, although she didn't really know who he was. It seemed that she just *liked* him. There was something about him that gave her a certain sense of peace that wasn't there when Marlena was in the room. There had been some oxygen loss to the brain and some head trauma in the accident that led to Abrie having to relearn basic day-to-day functions but the prognosis was favorable. She had friends and family praying for her, although she didn't recognize any of them. Her doctors were surprised at how well she was doing physically, in spite of her condition. They were talking of releasing her from the hospital to a rehabilitation center. There really wasn't much more they could do for her in the hospital since her life was no longer hanging in the balance. Her vitals were good, fluid levels were normal and she was physically doing well. With Marlena being the chief coroner for that area, Abrie was getting the best treatment money could buy. The move to the rehabilitation center was scheduled to take place over the next couple of days and her family and friends were excited about that.

SEVENTEEN

It had been a while since there'd been a girl's night out and China had called everyone to see if they wanted to plan one. Actually, since the night of the accident, the four friends had not been together in the same room. None of the girls were in the mood to party so they'd agreed to meet at China's house at the end of the week for a little get-together. As Damitria shopped for the food items they'd need, tears began to roll down her face. Although she'd known ahead of time, she couldn't believe her sister was dying. The test results showed an inoperable tumor at the base of China's brain and the prognosis was six months to a year, with two of the six months having already passed. Unbeknownst to her friends, China had planned to break the news to them at the gathering. Time was passing and she wanted to give them the opportunity to say proper good-byes. She wanted to be optimistic, but she knew her time had come and she was okay with that; sort of. On some days she did okay but on others, she'd break down crying hysterically. She knew that Angie would be okay, but she needed to be with her mother, not her aunt. She knew that Damitria would be okay but Angie was not her responsibility.

"Why, God? Why me? You know that my little girl needs a mother. Why are You doing this to her again? What kind of God are You?" China sobbed and sobbed. With the children being at the grocery store with Damitria, she could take advantage of the opportunity to let it all out. In front of her family, she was very strong. She didn't want them to know how scared she really was. What was death, exactly? We know that the body is placed in the ground and lowered or cremated but what happened after that? So many people had so many different ideas for answering that question, but who was right? What do people do? Pick the answer that best suited their needs and believed it? "God, how do we know? Are You really there? Who are You? Help me. Please help me to understand what's happening to me," she screamed just before burying her face into her pillow. Almost suddenly, she remembered the conversation she had had with Patricia on the night Abrie went to the hospital. Although she didn't understand it then, she was willing to give it another shot. She knew she needed something, and any little thing would help. She picked up the phone and dialed the number. The phone rang twice before the Reverend Boutier answered it. Before she knew it, she was crying in his ear. It seemed that the sound of his voice triggered a crying spell and she ended up telling him all about what was going on with her. He agreed to meet with her at her apartment later that evening. China planned to send her sister, nephew, and daughter out to dinner for the evening because she didn't want them to see her in the condition she knew she'd be in. When her sister returned home, she told her the plan and Damitria agreed to take the children out for pizza.

When Reverend Boutier arrived, China wanted to change her mind and send him home because she felt very awkward. She'd lived more than two and a half decades and had never called on God, so why call on him now that she knew she was dying? I mean, that's what most people did, but did He hear them? It almost felt like she was "pimping" Him. She wondered whether or not it was too late, or if He'd scoff at her with a "so-now-you-need-Me" attitude. Reverend Boutier assured her that God was not like that. He told her many things about God that she'd never heard before. Like the fact that God has feelings which make Him laugh when things are funny to Him and that He grieves when things go bad for the people He loves. She also learned that some people have the ability to hear Him speak. That one was kind of wild to her. God actually speaks? This *Being* who many people question the actual existence of has the ability to speak? That was a little too deep for her but the Reverend Boutier was very convincing. How do you know when He speaks? How do you know when it's Him?

She found herself pondering those two questions long after the Reverend left. The time they spent together was well worth it and she was left with a strange but wonderful sense of peace. Peace because she thought he was going to preach to her and read her last rites, but he didn't do any of that. He seemed to have an understanding of God that was all new to her. She'd never before heard the kinds of things he talked about, but what was quite interesting was that it was all believable. You could tell that the Reverend believed in what he was saying and he didn't get up and ask her for money before he left. He left her with an excitement that made her want to know his God, and that took her mind off dying--at least until now. She had forgotten about her situation and the reason for him coming over to spend time with her until now. Immediately, she began to panic. Somehow, she had forfeited her peace. She found herself lying in bed with tears welling up in her eyes as a barrage of questions about what she was going to do in her situation seemed to attack her. The attack came all at once, and from out of nowhere. She didn't sleep much that night. She thought about calling Patricia's dad back over but decided against it, thinking it would be too much at one time. She thought about attending his church but decided against that because people would think she was some hypocrite who was only there because she was dying and she didn't want that.

After almost an hour, she turned to look at the Bible that the Reverend had given her, which she'd placed on her nightstand. She wanted to read it but thought God would frown at her because of her last ditch efforts to call on Him. She had sinned too much in her day for Him to even consider hearing from her, so she stared at it for almost another hour. Suddenly, the urge to pick it up hit her. For a second or two, she thought she'd lost her marbles, but she couldn't shake the feeling so she picked it up and opened it. Not knowing what to read, she glanced down at the page in front of her and began on the red words where her eyes fell:

"But the tax collector dared not even lift his eyes toward Heaven as he prayed.

Instead, he beat his chest in sorrow, 'Oh God be merciful to me for I am a sinner'.

I tell you, this sinner, not the Pharisee, returned home justified before God. For the proud will be humbled and the humble will be honored." (Luke 18:13-14)

China couldn't believe her eyes! It was as if someone had been listening to her thoughts and knew exactly what she should read! She celebrated that for a few minutes, then wondered if it could have been more than mere coincidence. Could it have been? It was too perfect. God must have been listening! But why would he listen to me? One of the last things she remembered the Reverend having done before leaving was encouraged her to go to God to see what He would do. He gave her the Bible and told her that God could speak to her through it; "after all, it is *His* word."

China's mind started racing. The excitement of it all took her mind back to her conversation with Patricia at the hospital. It wasn't too late for Abrie so maybe it wasn't too late for her, either. Maybe He'd give her a second chance just as He'd done Abrie. I mean, after about six weeks, Abrie woke up. Maybe this was just to wake her up, too. Her excitement grew. She wanted to go and wake up Damitria, but she didn't. It was almost 2:00 a.m., and she figured her sister was tired after having had a night out with both children by herself.

Damitria lied awake in her bed. She couldn't sleep because she was worrying about her sister. How was China going to handle death? She didn't even seem interested in talking about God whenever she approached the subject with her, so Damitria was wondering if her sister was ready. She prayed and prayed, "God, please reveal Yourself to my sister. Don't take her without her knowing who You are. Yes, God, she is a sinner, but we all sin and fall short of Your glory. God, I know You're here because You've sent angels to talk to Angie, and You've given me peace about what is going to happen to my sister, but please don't just be here for Angie and me. Be here for China, too. She needs You now and so do we. God we need Your strength. Please save my sister, in the name of Jesus. Amen."

She thought to go to her sister's room and pray over her, but didn't. She also thought to anoint her sister's room with oil when she got up but thoughts of whether or not she'd been there for her sister spiritually rang in her mind. Silently, Damitria began to cry.

"Was there more that I could have done? Maybe I should have pushed and *made* her want to talk about You. I knew better, didn't I? Why didn't I sit her down and make her understand who You are? Is she going to die without knowing You now? Will You ever forgive me?" At that, Damitria cried herself to sleep.

The sun came up a few hours later. China and Angie were up with it, while Daniel and Damitria slept. "Mommy, Mommy!" Angie screamed.

"Let me guess. You want pancakes for breakfast, don't you?" she returned.

"Yep!"

"Yep?" China asked with that stern mother look on her face.

"I mean, yes ma'am," Angie said lowering her head.

"Now that's more like it," China said as she scooped her up with one arm and placed her in a dining room chair.

"Pancakes it is, Madam."

"Mommy, I really like pancakes," Angie said with a larger than normal smile.

"Little girl, you are going to turn into a pancake one of these days," China said as she tickled Angie who shrieked with laughter.

Around the corner, Damitria, who had suddenly awakened, listened quietly as her sister and her niece played together happily. She decided not to interrupt them, as they needed as much time together as possible. Damitria went back to her room and began to plan for the upcoming event. She'd promised her sister help with the preparations before leaving with the kids to go to their mother's house. Again, she began to cry. She missed her sister already and didn't know how to handle the last few months they'd have together. She had to decide whether to get closer to her best friend and sister, or to pull away from her, which was a much tougher decision than she'd ever imagined it could be.

EIGHTEEN

Ross jumped out of bed when the alarm went off and headed straight for the shower. This was the day his "baby" was going to be moved from the hospital to one of the best rehabilitation centers money could pay for. The apartment he was renting, which happened to be in a building owned by his brother Amos, was some distance from the hospital and he wanted to be there before Marlena pulled one of her stunts. He'd about had it with her by now. She kept insisting that they talk and try to work things out but Ross needed time and wasn't going to discuss it with her or anyone else before he was ready. He had been pushed around for more than ten years with everybody effecting the decisions he made. This time around, he was going to make his own decisions, in spite of what anyone else had to say about it because he'd finally realized that he was the one who would have to deal with the consequences. Part of the reason it was taking so much time for him to be ready was because he was celebrating his newfound autonomy. He was like a teenager who had been given a second chance to become a man and he was going to take his time to do it right this time. The truth be known, he harbored resentment toward Marlena for having pushed him around for so long and he wanted to punish her for having done so. She needed to suffer, and you could see that she was doing just that. She looked as if she hadn't been eating or sleeping, but it served her right. She wanted to be the boss. In their marriage, she was the man and the woman. "Let's see how much man she has in her now," Ross said aloud. He laughed as he got into the shower and felt the hot water pelting his scalp and his neck. He felt exceptionally good this morning and wasn't going to let anything steal his joy.

Upon arrival at the hospital, he spotted Marlena getting out of her car and was overjoyed that she had not beaten him there. She looked thin and sort of ragged. Ross smiled at that and said aloud to himself, "You're not so strong after all, are you, Marlena?"

He skipped a little as he hurried in to see Abrie. It was her breakfast time and he wanted to be the one to feed her. He enjoyed their time together even though she seemed to be like an eighteen month old child. It was as if he'd been given a chance at having small children of his own, and in therapy, she responded well to him. It was thought by the therapists that her response to him was due to the fact that he was as gentle with her as one would be with a baby. He didn't feel the need to rush her, which is what he anticipated from Marlena. Heaven forbid the chief coroner have a daughter who had a problem of some sort. How would that look to people? That might tarnish her perfection, but as long as Ross was around, no one was going to rush Abrie. She had been through enough.

When he got to her room, Abrie was sitting up in bed staring out the window. She turned to him and smiled as a toddler does upon seeing someone he loves. Though she didn't recognize him as the father she'd had for the last ten years, she did recognize him as someone she enjoyed spending time with. He was there every day and spent a lot of quality time with her. Most of the time, even during Marlena's scheduled feedings, Ross stayed there to support her. Marlena tended to be somewhat impatient and unkind whenever Abrie would not eat or abruptly stop eating in the middle of a feeding, and Ross was not going to allow her to hinder his daughter's progress in that or any other way.

Abrie was his life and he vowed to care for her as if she were his own. Marlena, however, was not as committed. She would come over on her lunch hour to tend to Abrie. Usually preoccupied with work, she'd try to force Abrie to hurry and eat--as if she couldn't take a longer lunch hour if she wanted to. She always watched the clock to make sure she didn't go over the allotted fifty minutes as, according to her calculations, it took her at least ten minutes extra minutes to get back to her office. On more than one occasion Ross had to take over. Once again, Marlena allowed work to interfere with the time she should have been spending caring for her child.

What Ross didn't know was that since Marlena's admission to the hospital, she had been seeing a therapist to help her to untangle her inner feelings. Ross proudly attributed her weight loss and lack of sleep to the fact that he wasn't living in the house with her. Marlena secretly appreciated the time she had alone but, at the same time, she felt she needed someone there to console her after each difficult session. It seemed that all of the loved ones in her life were either gone or so far away from her that she couldn't reach them. Because she'd abandoned them for so long, she didn't know how to reach out to them to apologize or to ask them to come back to her. She had to deal with the tragic death of her late husband which is what put her feelings on ice in the first place. She also had to deal with the fact that her father had abandoned her at a young age when he decided that life was "too hard for a man that young to have a wife and children". He walked out on her mother who had to fend for five young kids on her own. Marlena watched as her mother struggled and struggled to make the money they needed, but the ends never seemed to meet. Her mother would often emphasize the importance of education and how unimportant it was to have a man to depend on. She'd say, "The more education you have, the less you need a man around. Don't depend on a man to do anything for you because you are not promised that he'll stay. If he leaves you, like your daddy left me, then you'll be stuck, like me. If you don't want this kind of struggle, make sure you put yourself in a situation to take care of yourself with or without him."

Marlena had never forgiven her dad for having left the family; especially when she'd see him wining and dining other women, who were usually much younger than he. She had never forgiven her mother for having let him get away with it. Her mother never pursued child support or any kind of assistance from him. It was as if he'd gotten off scot-free and her mother wasn't woman enough to make a man out of him. She'd never forgiven Reggie for being so irresponsible, even after she pleaded with him to stay away from motorcycles. She hadn't forgiven him for leaving her with his three children to raise. In her eyes, he wasn't much better than her father but by the same token, he was the best thing that had ever happened to her. She hadn't forgiven Ross for not being man enough to stand up to her and put her in her place as a woman and a wife. She ran over him in the worst of ways and she resented the fact that he would set no boundaries. She hadn't forgiven herself for letting Reggie take that fatal trip, for allowing her children to grow up with no father, for allowing her husband to become her son or for allowing herself to curl up so tightly in a corner that she didn't know how to come out of it. She needed to forgive everybody, but she also needed to work through all of her other situations because they made her angry. They made her angry and by now, she was mad at the world.

When Marlena entered the hospital, she went into Abrie's room for just a few minutes. After having spent some time with her, the Patersons left to take care of the business necessary for having their daughter moved. That end of it took nearly an hour but they were satisfied with the outcome. The rehabilitation center staff transported Abrie to their facility. Ross and Marlena followed the van to the center in separate cars. There they were introduced to the team of people who would be working closely with Abrie. In spite of all of the negative feelings he had for Marlena, Ross was glad she was who she was because he believed her position and influence had a lot to do with the kind of treatment they were getting--as well as the service he knew was in store for Abrie.

After Abrie was settled in, Mr. and Mrs. Paterson went their separate ways with the promise of returning the next day. Abrie seemed to adjust well. With the wonderful team of physical, occupational, recreational, speech and other kinds of therapists and assistants to help her, she was like a toddler with lots of caretakers. The rehab center had a stellar reputation and was known for hiring the best in the country. It was no surprise that there was not a bad apple in the bunch.

The main goal of the therapy was, of course, recovery, but getting the family involved in the process was equally significant. This was of extreme importance to Abrie's recovery, which turned out to be a pretty speedy one considering the circumstances. Generally she responded well to the therapeutic techniques, especially to the therapists who were gentle and loving. There were, however, occasions when Abrie didn't want to do what she was asked and although she was usually easy going, she could be rather stubborn when she wanted to be. It seemed the only thing that would work in a situation like that was a call to or a visit from Ross. It became apparent, in a short period of time, that these episodes or set-backs tended to take place during or shortly after a visit from Marlena. Though Abrie was not yet talking, she did make noises at times that sounded very much like a preverbal toddler. As time progressed, Abrie began to smile as she pointed at what she liked and fold her arms and frown at what she didn't like. Words were obviously not what she needed in order to communicate. She really liked to play but what she liked more than that was water. She loved to splash in the water and was never a problem when bath time rolled around. Well, she wasn't *usually* a problem. As long as Ross was near, there wasn't a problem at all. But because of her age, Ross wasn't comfortable being in the room when she was being bathed and he certainly objected to any inkling of bathing her himself so often, Marlena was involved in that procedure. At times, she didn't want Marlena to touch her. She'd protest in an audible but nonverbal way and she certainly got her point across when she needed to. On a couple of occasions, Marlena was asked to leave, which never resulted in any kind of objection from her. She almost seemed relieved--as if she wanted them to finally give her a reason to not show up.

On the day she failed to show up, Ross blew a gasket. He was careful not to explode in front of Abrie but it was obvious that she sensed a problem. She withdrew from him when he tried to touch her and folded her arms and frowned. She was not cooperative at all on that day and, though Ross stayed with her for most of it to get her to cooperate with the staff, he eventually gave up and went home. For the life of him, he could not figure out what was so important to Marlena that she could miss the family therapy session. It really shouldn't have come as a surprise because, by now, he couldn't put anything past his selfish, self-absorbed, estranged wife. He called her from his cell phone and got no answer. He called her job to find out if she had taken time off, only to discover that she'd left work a little early. He completely dismissed the probability of her having been in a car accident. He would have known immediately if the chief coroner had needed medical treatment. He called their home several times but to no avail. He considered for a second, and then absolutely refused to go over to their house to check on her. All he knew was that Marlena had better had an awfully good explanation for why she wasn't where she was supposed to be.

His mind ran wild with the litany of possible selfish things she could have done. It would not have been beyond Marlena to have scheduled an appointment which she thought was more important than the recovery of her daughter. Surely, he thought, being chief coroner was much more attractive, important and appealing to her than being the mother of a young adult who had the mind of a child. Ross burned in his fury to the point of momentary insanity. (The things he wished on her were not clean enough to write in this book so they were left out!) Upon returning to his apartment, he slammed the door shut, never again to reopen it for the rest of the day.

What he didn't know was that if he had driven by his house, he would have found Marlena's car outside. If he'd gone into the house, he would have been able to follow Marlena's tracks to the basement where she had gone to visit a stash that had been kept neatly in an area down there, unbeknownst to him, for years. In it were all of the possessions Reggie Lofton had with him on that fateful day; everything down to the blood-stained cowboy boots he'd been wearing. Marlena had held on to as much of Reggie as she possibly could.

When she'd gone to her therapy session that day, she was mentally and emotionally brought back to the day it happened and told that she must let go of him and move on. She'd been told this several times before by different people, but she'd dismissed them all as ignoramuses that didn't know their heads from holes in the walls and she'd cut them all off as possible future conversation partners. But this time was different for her. This time she agreed that it was truly time to let him go. She'd learned in therapy that she'd passed up more than a decade of chances to love and be loved by others. She was finally able to see how it had ruined her life and damaged the lives of her family members. In the session she had become so angry at Reggie that she began to scream and cry uncontrollably. She blamed him for every bad thing that had happened to her since "he left". She blamed him for Abrie's accident, for her failing marriage, her distant sons, her lack of desire to meet and keep any friends and the fact that she was a workaholic. She even blamed him for the fact that her daughter, "who needed at least one (of us)", was adversely reacting to her when she went to see her. "It's your fault, Reggie," she screamed. "It's your fault that she doesn't like me. It's your fault that I don't like her. She wanted you to have that motorcycle! She thought it was so grand that 'Daddy' had such a 'big bike that made lots of noise'! She didn't discourage you and you encouraged her. I hate you for that, Reggie Lofton. I hate you, I hate you, I hate you..." she screamed as she sobbed and sobbed and sobbed. The session was so emotional that the therapist was nearly in tears.

After leaving the session, she called in to her job, took the afternoon off, and went straight home and into the basement. She spent the rest of the afternoon and the entire evening surrounded by the belongings of the late Reggie Lofton.

NINETEEN

CHINA LIED IN BED REFLECTING back on the last "Girls Night Out" gathering she and her friends had had. There's something about telling people that you're dying that scatters them like flies. You'd think they'd ban together and come closer to you, but as she found out that night, death and dying really and truly scares people away. It had been about two months since she'd seen her friends together. Every now and then one would trickle in and visit, but the stay wouldn't be long. Once in a while she got the dry "how-are-you-feeling-today" phone call from one of them, but those never lasted long either. It was as if they thought her tumor was going to jump on them through the telephone. She remembered pondering the things she'd said to them that night, trying to analyze them to find out where she'd fallen short with them. They had far too many memories for them to, all of a sudden, have nothing to talk to her about. It was as if all the fun and good times they'd had over the years had been blotted out because she was dying. In a nut shell, they'd all abandoned her--with the exception of Patricia. Patricia stayed around but got on her nerves with all of the Jesus stuff. I mean, it was okay but sometimes she seemed to go way overboard. It wasn't like hearing it from her father, who'd visit regularly once a week. China not only looked forward to his visits but was attending his Sunday morning worship services as well as the Wednesday night Bible studies. The truth was that she started doing this in hopes that God would make the tumor go away, but she found the information to be uplifting and interesting. This came as a shock even to her because she'd always been turned off by church people. They'd always seemed so phony to her, and the truth of the matter was that most them really were. The difference with Reverend Boutier was that in his church, you actually learned about life. There were no "hooping-hallelujah-feel-good" services. This man actually taught those interested about who God really is. She'd learned about the different names of God and what they meant. She'd learned to pray God's word back to Him and not stand in front of the congregation saying the same things over and over like most people did when they called themselves praying. She learned to ask for the things of God when she prayed because He already had knowledge of what the world needed; so instead of praying that He provide her with a car, she prayed His will for her life be done. She learned that God already had a plan and that it was "good that one should hope and wait quietly for the salvation of the Lord." Though she was learning a lot, she still struggled with the idea that people inside the church were judging her. The reality of it was that some were and some weren't. As good as the teaching was, there were members of his congregation that were still broken in spirit. She wasn't the only one there in need of help; many were in need of mental and emotional healing, as was she, and when that's the case, room for improvement is always present. Some of the females there were not sad about her cancer because it took away from her beauty. That made them feel more secure in their relationships with their men, but there were others who weren't distracted by her presence at all. They genuinely attended to get closer to God. She didn't feel out of place around them. In fact, she fit right in because they comforted her and let her know that they were happy to have another "sister" join. They welcomed her to share with them the beauty of God's love. These people weren't sickening like Patricia who seemed to be rehearsing her salvation speech.

China's thoughts were interrupted by Damitria calling to her to let her know that Patricia was on the phone. For a split second, she wondered if she should even take the call. Then she quickly remembered her first thoughts of the day which were about her "friends" having abandoned her; every one of them with the exception of this one. Then she wondered if it were really worth it to take the call because chances were high that she'd be bored with it any way.

"Hello," China said when she picked up the receiver.

"How's my sister in Christ today?" Patricia answered.

"I'm fine," China said rolling her eyes.

"You know today is the day for the church bazaar. If you feel up to it, I'll pick you and the kids up and we can go."

"No thanks," China responded.

"Well, I can understand. You must not be feeling well. Are you tired?"

"No. Actually, I'm just not in the mood for a church social," China said surprising herself and Patricia, too. "And do you want to know something else, Trish? I'm pretty tired of being your 'sistah in Christ'. That is not what you called me before I got sick so why don't I have a name, now? Why do you keep dumping this 'Christ stuff' on me? Is it because you didn't have a chance to make Abrie a 'sistah' before she became disabled? Is that it? I am sick and tired of you guys treating me like I'm a leper or something. Either your conversation has completely changed since finding out about my illness or it has ceased altogether. I don't need you all to tip toe around my illness and I certainly don't need you trying to redeem yourself through my situation."

"Did I catch you at a bad time?'

"No. Actually, you caught me at a good time because if I die tomorrow, unlike my best friends, I will not have to regret having been dishonest with you about how I feel about you," China screamed.

"You know something, China? You're not the only one who has problems around here, and your illness certainly doesn't give you carte blanche to treat people any old kind of way. Maybe you've changed, too. Have you checked your attitude lately? You're always down and trying to cheer you up is a chore. You're not the same person you were before the discovery of your illness, either. What are we supposed to do? Is it that *we're* acting like it's leprosy, or is it possible that we've all been affected by it, too? When you're about to lose one of your best friends, you have to figure out how you're going to handle it. You've got to prioritize things by their importance because you may not get to finish the list before you get the news that your girl is gone! I've noticed that you withdraw when I start talking about Jesus, but maybe it's not about you. Maybe this one *is* about me. Is that so wrong? This is how I choose to deal with losing you. I'll know that I did all I could for you," Patricia snapped back. "And don't call me 'Trish'. You know I don't like that name. Now, do you want to go to the church bazaar or not?"

After a couple seconds of silence, China said, "Sure. I guess I could go but the children are not going to be here. Damitria is taking them to a birthday party later on."

"I'll be there in two hours. Have your butt ready," Patricia said with authority and hung up the phone.

China was more than surprised by Patricia's way of handling the issue. Although she didn't know what she'd expected her to do or say, she knew she hadn't expected the reaction she'd gotten. She couldn't remember a time before when Patricia had been so assertive. After reflecting back on the conversation for a few moments, China chuckled to herself and said aloud, "well, I guess I'd better get up and get my 'butt' ready!"

On the other end, Patricia was also surprised by her reaction but felt a little victorious at the same time. Unbeknownst to the others, Patricia had always felt pushed around by them. At times, they took her kindness for weakness and seemed to think that because she was a preacher's kid, she was supposed to always turn the other cheek. There had been a few times, she remembered, when she attempted to assert herself. Each time, one of them would make a comment about it just before they'd chuckle in unison. Patricia would always retreat and, for this reason, the others never took her seriously. They treated her as if she was an absolute dingbat and she was tired of it. Privately, she had decided not to take it anymore. When you have a friend get into a near fatal car accident and discover only a couple of months later that another has a terminal illness, you can't help but take a long, hard look at life. After some contemplation, you realize that, as Solomon said in Ecclesiastes, "it's all vanity. It's like chasing the wind". And life without God is meaningless. It has no purpose. That's why so many, many people lead such empty lives. It's also why people who seem to "have it all" destroy themselves physically, psychologically and/or spiritually. If the world had spiritual vision, they'd be able to see the walking dead that surround them. They are those who are only concerned with the things of this world: cars, money, houses and what other people have to say. They fail to realize that without love, joy, peace, patience, kindness, etc., they can't truly enjoy those things anyway. Without God, you are nothing, you will have nothing, and you'll never be anything that matters. You just lead a selfish life that leads to nowhere and no matter where you turn, you end up empty. "Humph, they'd better recognize the Most High God," Patricia said as she finished preaching to herself.

Patricia had realized that her number one priority was getting right with God. In order to do that, she'd have to stop trying so hard to be accepted because God's people are *not* accepted by the world. The world finds God's people to be boring and ignorant because they don't gossip, cheat, lie, steal, backstab, envy, murder, and above all, they stay away from sexual immorality. It's not that they don't ever have to deal with those things because Lord knows they do. The difference is that they aren't proud of themselves when they fall, and they try to live a life free of those things because they don't *want* to grieve the Holy Spirit. Worldly folks think He's not looking but He is. "He sits high and looks low," she said aloud as she got out of bed and headed toward her closet to pick out an outfit for the day. She was going to have a blessed day in spite of any mood or attitude China was going to have and had declared that China would have a good day, too. Patricia knew that in order for that to happen, she'd have to pray before even picking her friend up. So that's what she did. After she finished, she showered, ate and started the journey to China's place.

TWENTY

THE SOUND OF THE CAR pulling up caused her to jump up and run outside. When she got to the driveway she screamed, "Daddeeeeee".

He got out of the car and hugged her as tightly as he could without cracking a couple of her ribs, kissed her on the cheek and said, "What's up, my angel?"

Angel, she thought to herself. She hadn't heard him call her that in years but she realized now that it was because she'd been acting like such a devil.

"Daddy, I'm so glad you made it. Where's Mom?"

"I tried to get her to come but she suggested the two of us spend time together alone since this is to celebrate us; just me and my baby. I took her up on that offer since it's been a long time since we've spent any quality time together. The fact of the matter is that, even though I rarely admit it, I do need the time away from everything. God knows I need a break. It didn't hit me until I began the drive up here."

"By the way, Daddy, how was the drive up?"

"It was very peaceful," he said as the two of them started up the walk. "The weather was good and the road was clear. It felt like I was one with nature."

As they walked in her front door she asked, "Are you hungry?"

Before he could answer, he looked up and saw a catered brunch with all the fixings. There were waffles with fresh strawberries and whipped cream, bacon, eggs, sausage; crab, potato, and macaroni salads, thinly sliced deli meats, fresh breads and rolls, fresh fruits and vegetables with dipping sauces, and an array of juices from fresh squeezed to concentrated mixes. His eyes widened and he gasped in delight exclaiming, "What did you do?"

"I had brunch catered for my daddy. Now, what would you like first?" she asked him as she escorted him to his seat. Even though it had been a long time since they'd spent any real time together, no one would have noticed. They laughed and joked, talked and sang and even prayed together. Nancy was thankful to God that He'd spared her relationship with her father. Though they never talked about the incident, it was understood that Nancy wanted forgiveness and that her dad had granted it. She told him about her friends, the accident, the coma, the rehabilitation and the tumor. *The tumor*, she thought to herself as she realized that it had been a while since she'd talked to China. She promised herself that she'd call her later to see how she was doing. She continued to spend quality time with her father, who not only needed it, but appreciated it very much.

The honking horn made more than a statement. China knew that not only was Patricia outside and ready to go, but that she was in an assertive stance that said, "Get yourself out here in a hurry because I'm not in the mood for foolishness. I'm not feeling sorry for you. You have a tumor; you're not an invalid. Without the tumor, I wouldn't get out of my car and come to the door, and I'm not getting out of my car to get you now, either. You knew I'd be here and you'd better be ready!" She couldn't have been further from the truth. As she was coming out the door, Patricia blew the horn one last time and yelled, "Hurry up, Girl. I've got things to do and I don't have all day." It was as if the previous conversation between them released Patricia to be who she'd always wanted to be on the inside. It was as if China had given her the permission the others had so denied her. The chatter in the car was reminiscent of old times--sort of. It resembled good times of the past between the five of them but it was different for Patricia. China found herself marveling at the fact that she had so many words inside her, for she was usually the quiet one. All of a sudden, it dawned on her that the two of them had never spent any time alone together. This was new and a lot of fun, as China would find throughout the progression of the day. They attended the church bazaar for a few hours, went shopping for another few hours, and went out to dinner and to a movie. It turned out to be a full day and it was thoroughly enjoyable for the both of them. By the time China got home, she'd found herself extremely exhausted. It seemed to hit her as soon as she walked into her bedroom. The fatigue was such that her muscles seemed to weigh a ton and after she'd sat down on her bed, they began to ache terribly. It felt like her body was on fire as it wrenched with this unfamiliar pain. Somehow China knew that this was the beginning of the end. She wanted to call Damitria but she and the kids were in bed already. Strangely, China knew she needed to go through this one alone and, although she wanted to be afraid, she wasn't. There was a strange sense of comfort that let her know that all was going to be okay. The muscle groups in her legs and arms began to cramp up and spasm. It seemed that her body was spinning out of control and that the control dials were popping off, showing the springs underneath them as you'd see in a cartoon. Oddly enough, she found herself laughing about that part of it. She knew it would only be a matter of time before signs of the presence of cancer would start manifesting in other parts of her body. It was no secret to her that she was dying and she was no longer afraid. She had "made peace with her Maker and she was ready to go," as the old folks used to say. She had a living will and had made funeral arrangements behind the backs of her loved ones. She knew no one in her family would have been strong enough to do those things but knew they had to be done. The Reverend Boutier played a major role in helping her to take care of her business. In fact, he'd done a lot of it for her and kept his vow to keep her business confidential. He'd even helped her to keep her doctor's appointments and to pick up her prescriptions. Not even the sister who lived with her knew all of the things that were going on. China wanted her last days to be as pleasant as possible for everyone around her and so far, things had gone well. She didn't know how much more of this she could keep under her hat because she wasn't sure of things to come. Her doctor had warned her that she would probably become very ill before it was over. She didn't want that and asked the Reverend to pray over her, for her and with her--which he did with no qualms.

China remembered the doctor having told her to be careful not to overexert herself and the muscle spasms were letting her know that she'd done just that. She didn't have the strength she used to have and she was now well aware of that. "I bet I'll take it easy from now on," she said to herself. She wanted to go to the medicine cabinet in her bathroom to find some muscle relaxants or pain killers but found she could not get up. At times the pain became incredibly unbearable but she could do nothing about it. She cried, wanting to scream for help, but she knew there was none for her now. The time had come. She began to pray, remembering the scriptures she'd learned from reading the Bible and from studying with Patricia's dad.

Though it seemed to take most of the evening, she finally fell asleep. The sleep was very peaceful and the dream was heavenly. As she awakened the next morning, she remembered having been in a very beautiful garden. She also remembered having been with someone, but couldn't remember who it was. The person was very calm and soothing and seemed to be taking all of her pain away. In fact, there was no pain at all in the dream. She remembered telling him where the pain had been but it seemed to have gone by the time he got there. It was as if the pain had been in all her head and she was trying to convince him that it had truly been there. He was comforting her, letting her know that all was okay. Awakening from the dream was disturbing for her because the peace left with the dream and the pain, though not as strong as the night before, was still there. Still, she couldn't move. Fortunately, Damitria came in routinely to check on her. She knew the door would open soon with her sister on the other side of it trying to be as quiet as she could. She'd have to ask Damitria to retrieve the medication for her. She'd never had to take it before, but she knew she'd need it this morning to get out of bed and after what seemed like days, her sister finally tiptoed to the door and pushed it open.

"You checking to see if I'm dead?" she said and mustered a laugh that hurt.

"Ha, ha. Very funny. No I'm not checking to see if you're..." Damitria stopped dead in her tracks and gasped. China looked like a train had run her over. Her eyes seemed to have sunken deep into her face. Her hair looked like it had been thinning and she seemed pale.

"What's wrong with you? Do I look that bad?" China asked.

"The question is, what's wrong with you? Are you okay?"

"Actually Dee, I'm not," she said with a wince and a grimace, "but I will be if you go to the medicine chest in my bathroom and give me the five medicine bottles from the bottom shelf."

Damitria did as she'd been asked. She handed the bottles to her sister and walked briskly out of the bedroom and into the kitchen to get a glass of water for her. As soon as she was out of her sister's sight, her knees gave out on her and she nearly fell to the floor. She literally stumbled into the kitchen as she decoded what was no mystery; she'd seen death on her sister's face. The look of death was unmistakable and you didn't have to work in the medical field to be able to recognize it when it made its appearance. Damitria knew the time was near. She pulled herself together and hurried to take the water to her sister. When she returned to the room, China's body was erect and seemingly stiff as a board. It was obvious that she was experiencing immense pain but "where" was the question. The expression on her face was one that silenced any communication as she just needed to get through whatever was happening to her. Damitria felt helpless and the next few minutes seemed like hours. When China was able, she gestured toward the bottles of pills she needed opened and without saying a word, Damitria knew what to do. She opened the bottle of muscle relaxants and fed two of them with a drink of water to her sister. At that moment, their eyes made contact. China granted Damitria permission to let go of her and prepare to move on with her life. Damitria resisted and China reprimanded her; all in one glance without any words being spoken. It was understood that it was time for her to go and she wanted no backtalk.

TWENTY-ONE

THE VIEWING OF THE BODY was scheduled on a Friday night. Although Abrie didn't understand what was going on, her parents made the decision to bring her to pay her last respects to her late friend, China Renae Mason. In her last will and testament, she'd requested cremation. Her family did not agree but had to do what she'd asked. China wasn't even thirty years old and her youth made it very difficult for her family and friends. Abraham was a real help to Della, even with the serious issues he'd had to face in recent weeks. He and Della had grown really close and were spending a lot of time together, much to Greg's chagrin. Though surprised at his presence, none of the remaining friends verbalized their feelings about it. The Reverend Boutier officiated the services which proved to be a very emotional thing for him. He and China had grown close over the months before her death. She was like a daughter and it made him aware of the mortality of his own children. Patricia was the basket case everyone knew she'd be. She took it exceptionally hard. It was as if she hadn't had enough time to prepare for the loss of her friend. Truth be known, she never believed God would let China die and she was angry at Him because of it. She'd prayed and prayed for Abrie and it worked so she couldn't figure out why He didn't listen to her as she prayed for China. She felt she had failed her friend and because of it, she died. Nancy cried a lot but didn't say much. She hadn't kept the promise she'd made to herself to call her terminally ill friend to check on her. Before she knew it, it was too late. Nancy realized that China's illness made her think about her own mortality and she wasn't ready to do that. Being around China made her feel like she was around old people and that made her uncomfortable. Why hadn't she thought of her friend's discomfort? Why hadn't she thought about her friend at all?

"Anyone sitting here?" Greg asked, interrupting her thoughts.

"No," she said between sobs.

After about three minutes, Greg asked, "Nancy, who is that guy with Della?"

Nancy gave him a real hard look for a few seconds and said, "Greg, if that's why you're here, you may as well go home. As a matter of fact, why don't you just leave now?"

"My bad. I'm sorry. I know this is not the time for this but when a man sees his wife with another man he can't help but want to know who he is."

"Wife? Wife, Greg? Now she's a wife to you? I can't believe your nerve. Was she a 'wife' when you ran off with Shelda? Was she a 'wife' when you drained the bank account dry and the girls and I, including the one whose body is in the casket up there, had to help her to pay *your* mortgage, feed her and keep her lights on? Maybe the 'guy' she's with is the man you should have been when you were playing little boy games with your secretary!" At that, Nancy stood up and excused herself. Greg sat there looking as if Nancy had an attitude problem. He really didn't get it. As far as he was concerned, Della should have been sitting at home awaiting his return. What the girls didn't know was that he would often cry himself to sleep at night because he missed her so much. What he really missed was how she used to take care of him as well as the household responsibilities. Della never missed a beat. Whatever needed to be taken care of was handled properly as long as Della was around.

Ironically, that was what Abraham appreciated most about her, too. In recent weeks, Driscelle began showing her true colors. As soon as she found out Della existed, she seemingly lost her mind. She began knocking on his door at all times of the night, thinking she'd catch them in bed together. The truth of the matter was that Della respected his celibacy because she had come to the same place in her life. Neither of them wanted to desecrate the relationship by "stirring love before it awakened". Each of them wanted to enjoy the other and grow together in love with no distractions or interruptions. It just seemed to them that you could be more open and honest with each other as long as there was no sex involved. They also understood that sex would have left them with a false sense of each other and a false sense of themselves in the relationship so Driscelle was wasting her time and everyone else's.

Each time he'd go to the door to see what she wanted, she'd come up with something involving Little Abe. Once she went as far as to knock on his door at 3:56 a.m. to tell him that his son "missed him terribly and wanted to see him." She said the baby wouldn't go to sleep until he saw his daddy. Abraham knew it was a hoax and told her to hold him tightly and whisper to him that "Daddy missed him, too, and would see him at a decent hour when he knew he was really awake." With a strong show of anger, he slammed the door in her face. But before the door shut, he'd told her she needed to find herself a man so she could leave him alone, and that made Driscelle crazy. She began calling him from her cell phone. He knew it was her so he didn't bother to answer. When she reached her home, she called and called, obviously hitting the redial button without hanging up the receiver. This lasted for thirty minutes before he turned off the ringer to his phone, which he hated to do because he often forgot to turn it back on, resulting in missed phone calls. And that was how Della came to know about her.

Abraham's ringer had been off for two days before he realized it, and when Della couldn't get in touch with him, she thought the worse. Being crazy about the man, she thought she'd had some competition who had won, leaving her out in the cold. She just figured he didn't want to spend any more time with her but chose not to tell her. At that time, Abrie was still in the hospital and when Della went to see her, she ran into him. He thought it was that she didn't want to talk to him, so the moment was a little awkward for both of them until he asked her why she wasn't calling any more. It was then that he took the opportunity to tell her about Driscelle. Much to Abraham's surprise, Della wasn't turned off by the drama.

Not long after that, Della and Driscelle met. Abraham and Della were enjoying an evening cafeteria dinner when Driscelle walked up to their table pointing her finger in his face and rolling her neck for emphasis. Although her voice was louder than necessary, she was careful not to shout obscenities at him because she'd been escorted from the hospital for doing that once before and warned that if she'd ever done it again, she would be banned from the facility. She looked Della up and down and called her a really ugly name but before he could defend her, Della had it handled. With a smile and in a very calm tone of voice, Della told Driscelle that she'd "walked upon the wrong woman" for that kind of drama. Della let her know that in no way, shape, form or fashion would she allow her to disrespect her or Abraham, "publicly or privately", and if they needed to handle it as two women should, they could "take off their rings and get some Vaseline". That was the last time Driscelle ever addressed Della. Secretly, Abraham was very impressed. He knew Della could handle her business, which suggested that she was strong, and he longed for and needed a woman of strength. But now it was his turn.

As they left the building, Greg followed them out. He picked up his pace and stepped out in front of Della and grabbed her by the shoulder. "Della, we need to talk," he said in an extremely authoritative tone.

"Not tonight you don't," Abraham said with more authority.

"Man you need to handle yours so I can handle mine," Greg said.

"What you got here? You ain't got nuthin' to handle here man. If you gon' handle yours, I say you'd better find it first."

"Della..." Greg said.

Abraham stepped out in front of her and said, "The lady doesn't have anything to say to you tonight that she hasn't said before. If she did, she would have hit you on the hip a long time ago. Bruh, you'd better check your pager again. The number on it ain't hers. Now if you don't mind, *my* lady and I are leaving. Excuse us." Abraham pushed past Greg while staring him straight in the eye as if to let him know that it could be finished now or they could finish it later at the place of his choice. Abraham was obviously not going to back down, which caught them all by surprise. Even Della had him pegged as the hoity-toity type. He'd always used such perfect grammar with proper manners. This night he sounded straight from the hood. He had obviously not forgotten his roots. Secretly, she was impressed.

Greg was left standing with his manhood in his hands but he knew not to pursue this one. Part of him wanted to go after him but a bigger part of him encouraged him to cut his losses which wasn't easy for him. He wanted to call her, but couldn't, because he didn't have the phone number. He couldn't go and visit her because in the six months he'd been gone, she'd moved from the house they'd shared. She transferred to a different office, so he didn't even know where she worked. That was why he used to call Abrie. She was his only connection to her and now, that was gone. He sounded so pitiful, but all Della could do was put him on ignore—forever! It took some time but he eventually moved on. He didn't have any other choice. Sadly, the only reason he'd shown up to the viewing was because he knew she would be there. It's shallow but that's what desperation will do to a person.

Nancy collected herself enough to go over to the podium where Patricia and the Reverend Boutier were standing. She offered to give her a ride home because her father had to finish up with the family and take care of some other business that Patricia wasn't interested in being involved in. Because she was taking it so hard, Nancy knew she needed to go home. In fact, she was sort of making a fool of herself. No one can tell another the proper way to mourn, but Patricia just seemed to be going overboard. For someone who was usually so quiet, this girl was making a lot of noise that seemed so unnecessary. Nancy wondered for a minute whether or not the girl was embarrassing her father who was always so poised. Patricia accepted her offer and they walked out of the building together. It had been a rough night for everyone and they all needed some sleep.

TWENTY-TWO

SEEING CHINA'S LIFELESS BODY LEFT a stain on the brain of most of those who viewed it, but for Ross and Marlena Paterson, the experience proved life altering. Even though they weren't staying in the same house, they were similarly affected by what they'd seen. Though Ross knew the body belonged to China Mason, he saw Bianca Noland; Marlena saw Reggie Lofton. The experience drew them both closer to Abrie and her situation. Never again did Marlena miss another appointment to feed or bathe her daughter. She made it to all of the family therapy sessions, as did Ross for a while, but things were strained and strange between them. Anyone in close proximity could feel the tension between them but no one, including the two of them, could put his finger on the exact cause of it. Having each lost loved ones, and nearly losing another was only part of it. They had the issue of their marriage and the subsequent relationship to deal with. While in therapy or around therapists they never brought up the personal problems they were having, but that didn't make them go away. They were there hovering over the two of them and anyone else nearby. They had their jobs and other family concerns, but above all, unbeknownst to them, they needed to deal with themselves. The man and woman they were before their marriage were broken people who were never put back together. Half a man and half a woman in a marriage don't make a whole because marriage requires fullness from both parties so that one may supply the other's lack when necessary without losing himself. As in the current situation, neither of them could help the other because half of each of them had been taken to the grave by the previous partner and as a direct result of it, their marriage had fallen apart. Neither of them saw that until today. Today they witnessed, from a one-way glass, one of Abrie's rehabilitation sessions. In the session, Abrie had been given some paper, scissors, crayons and pencils and was asked to draw something. She had also been given some paper dolls with the option of using the figures to show the therapist what was on her mind. Abrie took the paper dolls and traced them on a stack of papers and very carefully, much to the amazement of all watching, cut them out. Taking her time, she carefully colored each one. When she'd finished, she held them up like a banner and what Ross and Marlena saw came as an absolute shock to them. The finished product showed a pattern of about four men and women connected to one another. The shock was that if you looked at any two of them at one time, they seemed to be either facing each other or walking away from one another! Maybe no one else could place a finger on what was causing the tension between Ross and Marlena, but Abrie could---

and did! Who would have suspected her as the one to pinpoint the actual problem? It seemed as though the message from the pattern was that a decision needed to made by the two of them to either stay together or to separate, but they couldn't straddle the fence as if the problem would fix itself. It almost seemed as if Abrie was trying to let them know that she was feeling the tension and didn't like it. Maybe they were reading too much into the project but nonetheless, they both walked away with the same message.

Abrie never made any other kind of suggestion or gesture about it after that. It was as if she'd checked out immediately after she'd given them the message she was sent to deliver, and when she made her point, it was over. That task was done.

The rest of the recreation therapy session went well. For that matter, the rest of her day went well. She was fully cooperative and seemed to enjoy all of her other sessions, as well as the rest of her schedule, but she certainly left a few people dumbfounded by the earlier event. No one knew what to say, and they knew better than to try to pull out of her what it all meant because she wasn't verbal yet. She could make sounds, some of which resembled real words, but she wasn't able to carry on a conversation. The recreation therapist sensed the same thing and as a result of it, she forwarded the pattern to the family therapist and asked that it be addressed in the family session scheduled for the next afternoon.

In the session, the therapist eased the Paterson/ Lofton family into the issue. As far as therapists go, this one was very smooth. Rather than bluntly asking about the family problems, she asked Ross to express how he'd felt about Abrie's progress. As he began to compliment her and the rest of the staff on the "superb" services, she thanked him as she asked him how he thought his daughter would do at home after having been released from rehab. His answers were very careful, but the therapist could see Marlena's tension building. As Marlena came closer to blowing, the therapist asked her how she thought the role of the family would benefit or hinder Abrie's rehabilitation. Just as she suspected, Marlena began to accuse Ross of hindering the process by seeing the world through rose colored glasses. She said he never answered any questions head on and that his indecision would hurt Abrie's progress just as it had hurt their marriage. Upon hearing that, Ross went nuts. At one point, he stood up and had to be asked to sit back down or leave. Though Marlena had never seen that side of him, she seemed to like it. Instantaneously, she began baiting him and then it slipped out.

"This would have never happened in the first place if you were more like Bianca," he screamed. "Why didn't I marry Bianca when I had the chance? What did I do to myself?"

As Marlena looked on in shock, the therapist asked, "Who is Bianca?"

Ross glared at the therapist for a few seconds, as if Bianca's name was sacred and shouldn't have been uttered by anyone but him. Marlena continued to look on as she waited for an answer. Ross obviously was not ready to talk because he stood up and excused himself before exiting the room. Abrie, who had been in there the whole time, seemed to tense up as the voices got loud but seemed to calm down as soon as everyone else did. She seemed to be in her own little world--until he walked out. She began pointing and went into hysterics until he came back into the room. She calmed down as quickly as she started up and settled into her world as if nothing had ever happened. Ross apologized for walking out so abruptly but didn't say much else throughout the remainder of the session. Marlena was also as quiet as a church mouse, mainly due to shock and curiosity about who Bianca was. Until now, she had never even heard this name. She wondered if this woman came before or after they were married. The look in her eyes revealed immense curiosity and deep wonder, but also fear. For ten years, she believed she was the cherry on top of his whipped cream. Now she questioned whether or not the cream was even whipped.

TWENTY-THREE

THE SOUND OF THE DOORBELL ringing brought Nancy back from the nostalgic place she had been in for the last fifteen minutes. The alarm had sounded, she'd hit the snooze button intending to rise and shine, but decided she'd take a few more minutes before getting dressed to go to work.

"Just a minute," she yelled. She jumped up and ran to wash her face, wondering who would be at her door at that time of morning on a week day. When she looked through the peephole, what she saw left her stunned and paralyzed for a couple of seconds. When she could move, she opened the door.

"Marlena, what are you doing here?" she asked.

"Nancy, I need to talk. May I come in?"

"Sure but I don't know how much time I have to devote to you this morning. I have to be at work in a couple of hours and I haven't even showered yet."

Pushing her way in the door, she bluntly asked, "Have you been seeing my husband?"

"I beg your pardon," Nancy said with wide eyes.

"I know it may come as a surprise to you coming from me but I'm not crazy. I know you've had a thing for Ross for a long, long time."

"Mrs. Paterson, do you see your husband here? For that matter," she said as she stepped aside, "do you see any evidence of your husband ever having been here and why are you at my house at this time of morning with this nonsense?"

"Nancy, Ross has not been home in months and I don't know where he's staying..."

"So you just assumed he'd be here? I think you'd better leave. I don't have time for this, nor will I entertain it any longer," she said as she showed Marlena to the door. "And by the way, if you'd be a little more sensitive and caring, you wouldn't have to look for your husband at another woman's place because he'd be at home with you, where he's supposed to be. I don't know where he is, he isn't here, and has never been here but if I see him, I'll be sure to tell him you're looking for him. Good day, Mrs. Paterson."

Marlena opened her mouth to say something but Nancy motioned toward the outside of the door and closed it as she walked out.

"The nerve of that woman," she exclaimed. "The unmitigated gall! The audacity!" After about ten minutes, she picked up the phone to call Della, but the doorbell rang again. She stormed to it, thinking it was Marlena. When she snatched it open, she couldn't believe her eyes. Not only could she not believe what she was seeing, but had difficulty believing the kind of morning she was having in general--especially after she'd only been out of bed less than thirty minutes.

"May I come in," Ross asked.

"No," Nancy came back.

Surprised at her response, he stood before her dumbfounded.

"What is this? A joke or a feeble attempt to set me up?" she asked him.

"I'm sorry. Did I wake you up?"

"No but your wife, who was here less than fifteen minutes ago, did. What is going on? Is she out in the car waiting for you?"

"No. I'm by myself..."

"If your wife is not with you then why are you here?" she snapped finding no humor in the situation and even less sensitivity.

"Marlena was here?" he asked with obvious astonishment.

"Mr. Paterson, I don't know what is going on but I really don't have time to play games with your wife or you. She was here about fifteen minutes ago asking me if I'd seen you. I told her I hadn't but if I did, I'd be sure to tell you that she was looking for you. Now, if you don't mind, I need to get dressed for work."

"I'm real sorry, Nancy. I didn't know she'd come over here and I'm sorry to have bothered you myself."

Nancy quickly analyzed the look on his face and his tone of voice. Realizing that he was really sincere, and that he was indeed shocked at finding out that his wife had been there, she looked around outside for Marlena's car. Feeling a little embarrassed while letting her guard down slightly, she asked, "How's Brie doing?"

"Uh, she's doing fine. She's okay, I guess."

The pitiful look on his face caused Nancy to relent. She opened the screen door and said, "Alright. Come on in but only for a few minutes because I do have to go to work."

Ross didn't hesitate or stutter step as he desperately accepted the seemingly long awaited invitation to enter into her domain. In twenty minutes he'd managed to fumble around and say nothing more than that he needed to talk to someone. He said he didn't know where else to turn and that he really didn't know why he'd come to her nor did he understand how his wife knew he'd be there that morning. Nancy's obvious impatience with the situation sent him on his way a lot sooner than he'd intended to go. She hurried to get dressed but couldn't wait to call Della to tell her what had happened. For some strange reason, Della didn't seem surprised. She didn't have much time to discuss it because she was running late for a breakfast date with Abraham. This made Nancy feel rejected, and she became resentful. Ever since he came into the picture, her "friend" didn't have time for her. They used to chat for hours on the phone each day, but all of a sudden, Della stopped calling and no longer returned her phone calls. "There's just something about him that I really don't like," she said to herself after hanging up the phone. "He's around a little bit too much for me. First dinner, then lunch and now breakfast, too? Wonder what he's running from. I mean the brother has a job, but why does he have so much free time?"

"Hey, you," Abraham said as Della sat down at his table.

"Hi," Della said just before greeting him with a kiss.

"I know you may be thinking this is a little bit much but I just had to see you this morning."

"If I thought it were too much, I wouldn't be here. You get no courtesy visits and I certainly don't feel obligated to be with you. Besides, you're paying," she said and they both laughed. Abraham had made very clear, on an earlier date, that she was "in no way, shape or form" ever to pay for a meal they had together. It was nice to know that chivalry was not dead in their relationship. "So what's on your mind," she asked.

"Not too much," he replied.

"Abraham, we haven't known each other long, but I've known you long enough to know that if you've invited me to breakfast there's something going on in that pretty little head of yours. Is it Driscelle and the baby?"

"You see, that's what I like about you. You seem to really know me," he said with a smile. "There is something on my mind but it's not Driscelle."

"So what is it?" she asked almost cutting him off.

"Della, I've been thinking..."

"Well, that's a relief," she interrupted and they both laughed.

"Ha. Ha. Very funny. I'll give you that one because this is serious; at least to me it is."

"Okay, I won't crack any more jokes or make any smart comments," she lied, and they both laughed again.

"You sure know how to take the edge off for a brothah. But on the serious tip, Del, I want to discuss something with you. I need your opinion but I need you to just hear me out first. Okay?"

"Oh, alright," she said. "I'll listen. Just don't come up with anything crazy."

He smiled a half smile before he began, which let Della know it was time to get down to business. "Del, I've been giving some serious thought to my paternity situation. For four years it never mattered to me but now, all of a sudden, it does. I was never tested because as I told you before, the boy needed a father. I've always felt he wasn't mine, but I knew he needed a dad so I just went with it. But since I've been with you, I've been seeing things in life differently. For the first time in four years, I actually feel violated. I feel like she stole something from me and, excuse me if this sounds crass, but I feel like I was robbed of my virginity. Being a father for the first time is sacred. It's something you can only do once, and I guess it didn't mean as much to me before because I never thought I'd meet anyone who I'd want to experience that with."

"Abraham, are you saying that you want to have children with me?"

"No. I mean, yes, but not right now. That is if you'd ever consider me as a father for your children."

"But we haven't even discussed marriage and I'm certainly not ready to take that step."

"Della, don't misunderstand what I'm saying. I'm not suggesting we go make a baby together. What I'm saying is that being around you makes me look at the world differently. Even if I don't have children with you, I now know the importance of being with the woman I love when I sire children," he said then looked away in silence.

After a few uncomfortable seconds, Della asked, "so what? Does this mean you're thinking of taking a paternity test?"

"Exactly. Don't you think I should?"

"Abraham, that's not my call."

"I'm not asking you to make the decision for me. That's been done already. I'm asking you to support me in my decision."

"So you want me to hold your hand as you do this, right?"

"Della, this isn't funny. I wish you'd get serious."

"I'm about as serious as I can be right now. What am I supposed to say?"

"Tell me whether or not it's the right decision."

"Why? It seems the decision has already been made."

"Maybe I shouldn't have said anything."

"Abraham, if you want me to encourage you, I will but not in the way you want me to. I won't encourage you to take the test or discourage you from taking the test. What I will do, however, is encourage you to do whatever you feel is right. I can't make this decision for you, nor am I in a position to influence your decision about it."

"I can respect that, and my decision is to go ahead with it. I'm just asking you to be there for me."

"What if you find out he's not yours? Are you ready for that kind of blow?"

"I'll just have to deal with it. You see, I've been running from the truth long enough and being with you makes me want to know whether he's really my responsibility."

"But you're the only father he knows. What are you going to do if you find out he's not yours? Leave him? You can't do that."

"No, I'm not going to desert the boy. Knowing his crazy mother, once she sees that she's not going to get what she wants from me, she'll find some new meat and move on anyway. In the back of my mind, I've always feared she'd take him away from me one day, sooner or later. In a sense, I distanced myself as a result of it. I know that cuckoo too well. She's always an hour ahead or an hour behind. Her time has never been right since I've known her."

"So why have you put up with this all these years?"

"Honestly, I think I felt guilty."

"Guilty?"

"I know this is going to sound crazy but my mother didn't raise me to take advantage of women. I should have never gotten intimate with her."

"Well, if I remember the story, you were the one being taken advantage of."

"I know but I should have made a more sound decision. I knew better but I didn't act like I did. But that's neither here nor there. I need to be a man and face this dragon. I've run from it too long and eventually the truth was going to come out and thanks to you, Del, I can do what I have to do."

"Does this make me a home wrecker?"

"Not funny."

"I guess that was done in poor taste, huh?"

"Speaking of taste, would you like to order some food? I'm hungry."

"Yeah, me too."

They ordered their meals but both felt a little awkward while eating. Abraham knew he'd already ordered the test and would be able to take it as early as that afternoon. That was one of the advantages of working for a hospital. You knew people who could hook you up with whatever you needed. Della felt awkward because she knew her mate was going to go through a major life change but wasn't sure whether or not he realized how this truth could change him forever. She believed he was only thinking of his relationship with her--at least, that's how it sounded from the conversation they'd just had. She knew he wasn't considering the bond he and the little boy had made over the years, or the anger he would possibly experience upon finding out that this woman had held him hostage for five years of his life after having been impregnated by another man.

TWENTY-FOUR

DRISCELLE ABOUT HIT THE CEILING when she received notice of the paternity test. In her mind, Della had to have been the reason for it. She was pacing the floor, cussing and throwing things around in her room when Little Abe came in and asked what was wrong. Rather than a show of affection, she screamed at him to leave her alone and to get out of her room. Of course he began to cry, and that made her even more furious. After calling him a few choice names and swatting him on the butt, she sent him to his room. She continued to pace the floor until a plan popped into her head. She had to get rid of Della. Della was causing way too many problems for her taste. She picked up the phone and dialed the number of an old friend.

"Yello."

"Fabian?"

"Yea. Who you be?" he asked demonstrating the good mood he was in.

"Fabian, this is Driscelle."

"Well, well. If it ain't 'Ol' Prissy Drissy'. What brings you back to the hood? You miss us folk down here?"

"Not really, Fabe. I need a favor..."

"Figures," he said cutting her off. "The last favor you needed from me has not been paid back yet, so what makes you think I'll do this one for you? The last favor got you out of the hood and you never looked back. You owe me, girl. What do you think I am? Your fool or something?"

"No, Fabe. It's not like that. Do you remember that favor you did for me?"

"Of course I remember. How could I forget? I was waiting for round two but you never showed up. You lied to me, girl. You had me waiting for you and you never showed up. It's hard for a brothah to forget something like that. What you did was cold. You left a brothah hanging and I had everything set up and ready for you."

"But Fabe, that was a long time ago. You can't find it in your heart to forgive a sistah?"

"Forgive? You must think ol' Fabe is stupid or something. You think you can play a playa like that? You wouldn't be thinking about forgiveness if you didn't need another favor. The only reason you're talking like this is because you want Fabe to do something else for you, but if it's anything like the last favor, you just might get it."

"Well, if you play your cards right, it just might be like the last favor."

"How do I know I can trust you? You said the same thing the last time. Drissy, you know a brothah had feelings for you, but you played me. You used me to get what you wanted and then you boned out. I'm not down this time."

"Meet me at Farlane's tonight and I'll tell you what I need."

"Farlane's? The old one or the new one on 98th and Adams?"

"The old one. Meet me around 7:30."

"Just like that. Ol' Fabe is supposed to just drop what he's doing to do what you want him to do? What's in it for me? Like I said, you haven't paid the last debt. You still owe me."

"I know and I'm ready to pay up."

"When?"

"Tonight when I see you."

"Wear something real nice."

"Just be there and on time. Don't have me waiting for you."

"I'll be there. You just be ready to pay up."

"Yea, whatever. We'll see how bad you want it," she said just before hanging up. She didn't even give him a chance to say "good-bye". She went to her lingerie drawer and pulled out something she knew Fabian would like. Fabian had always been easy for her. He would do whatever she told him to do at any cost. He wanted her just that much and she knew that was her hole card. She began celebrating with loud cheers and laughter. "You best watch your back, Miss Della. It's curtains for you. You'll think twice before you decide to sleep with another woman's husband--if there's anything left of you. Now let's see. What should Drissy have done to Della? Rearrange her face? Cut it off or just take her out?"

On the other side of town, Fabian was thinking about what he should do. Did he want to open up this can of worms again or not? The last time he did a favor for Driscelle, she left him hanging. That wasn't the first call he'd gotten from her since the last favor. She called and talked to him like he was nothing and he remembered what she'd said to him. She told him that he *was* nothing and *would never be* anything. She also said he wasn't good enough to shine the bottom of her shoes. He was "no Abraham" and he shouldn't ever think he could be. She'd graduated from the bottom where Fabian would always be and he shouldn't ever think he could touch her again.

She talked about him so badly that it hurt him for a long time. It hurt because he thought he really did love Driscelle. The fact that she wanted him to impregnate her for another man left him angry and confused. He thought the pregnancy would make her change her mind and the three of them could be a family. He figured her hormones were making her hateful and that she'd calm down eventually, but she never did. She was as mean and hateful as could be, but he loved her anyway. It seemed that every chance she got, she'd humiliate him in the worst of ways. She delighted in telling him he was not good enough for her and that if he were half the man Abraham was, he still wouldn't have a chance. She'd laugh in his face and tell him that he should stop trying to be with her. He thought about going to Abraham to tell him that the baby wasn't his, but he didn't know him. The other side of that problem was that he hated Abraham with every fiber of his being because he had what Fabian so desperately wanted. Without any effort, Abraham made him feel less of a man and he resented that. At one point, he thought of killing him but he couldn't, for some reason, bring himself to do it. One night after Driscelle belittled him to tears, he grabbed a six pack and his glock and headed over to the hospital to wait for Abraham's shift to end. He was going to ambush him and this "god" of Drissy's would never have known what hit him. He'd only seen Abraham from a distance so he really didn't know what he looked like. That was part of the reason he didn't kill him. He waited in the hospital parking lot for about three hours before he decided to go back home. What he didn't know was that Abraham wasn't at work that night anyway.

It took him a long time to get over the heartache of losing Driscelle to some uptown college boy but after a few years, he managed to get over it. Right now, he was wondering whether or not he should open up that can of worms again. He knew she was a user and that once she got what she wanted, she'd put him down and stomp on his heart the way she did before. There was also the fact that he was married now with a baby of his own on the way.

"Hey, Baby. What cha thinkin' bout?"

"Oh, hey, Babe," he said as he received the hug she reached out to give him.

"You look like there's something real deep on your mind," said Atina, who was once Driscelle's best friend. In fact they had been buddies until Driscelle moved uptown and decided she was better than the rest of them. The truth of the matter was that Abraham had moved her out of the "hood" in an attempt to help her since she was having his baby.

He'd helped her to find a decent job and took care of her financially until she got on her feet. During those days, they thought they were going to get married, but they didn't.

When Driscelle started acting different, Atina and Fabian got together just to console each other but found out they had more in common than they'd thought. They'd gotten together shortly after Driscelle found out she was pregnant and had been together ever since, unbeknownst to Driscelle. They both knew she'd have a hissy fit upon finding out that her old "stash" was no longer available for her use and that the reason was because of her old buddy Atina. But for the two of them, there was some kind of sweet enjoyment in her finding out.

"Guess who just called me for a favor?"

"Who?"

"Your buddy, Driscelle."

"What?" she asked insecurely.

"Yea, there's something she wants me to do. She wants me to meet her tonight at the old Farlane's at 7:00."

"You going?"

"I don't know."

"What do you mean you don't know? After all she did to you, why would you even consider it? You know she only wants to use you for something. Baby, you have just straightened up your life. Things are going good for us. Please don't do anything stupid."

"What are you really worried about, Tine? Is it me going back to jail or is it that some old feelings will come up between us?"

"Baby, you know I don't want to lose you. I love you and things are going fine for us. I don't want you to go to her or to jail."

"I love you, too, Baby," he said as he caressed her knees and kissed her in the mouth.

"So what are you going to do?"

"I don't know. What do you think I should do? What if she really needs something?"

"Let her wonder boy hook her up. Matter of fact, I have an even better idea. Why don't we go together? We'll give Miss Thang a taste of her own medicine. She's always playin' folks. It's time to play a playa," she said, and they both laughed and agreed upon this being the best way to deal with Driscelle.

Inside, Fabian was trying to fight what he thought were his true feelings. He knew he loved Atina because she'd been there for him through thick and thin, but he'd never had any closure with Driscelle. He did understand one thing, though; Driscelle always left him with his heart in his hands and Atina was faithfully there every time to pick up the pieces.

Atina understood the same thing. She knew Driscelle was stiff competition but she loved Fabian. They had something good and she was not about to let her old friend mess that up. Nor was she going to stand around and watch as the girl destroyed her husband emotionally just so she could put him back together again. She'd had enough of this "Humpty-Dumpty" stuff. Atina was ready to fight this time. She left Fabian sitting on the bed and went to the bathroom to have a good cry. She knew the time would eventually come when she'd have to face Driscelle and her relationship would be put to the test but, the truth be known, she was scared. In her heart, she'd always felt that Fabian loved her and would never let her go. She knew she was number two and somehow she had accepted that. Deep down inside, she'd hoped Abraham and Driscelle would make it so Fabian could be all hers. When she found out they didn't get married, Atina was devastated. Actually, she was happy about that, too. She wanted Driscelle to hurt and to hurt badly, because she'd grown to hate her for all of the things she'd done to the people around her. Especially Fabian. It was because of Driscelle that he'd had so much pain and when he went to jail for assault and battery, it was her fault. If he hadn't been walking around with so much pain inside him, he would have never beat down that old man. She made him the monster he'd become over the years and he's finally able to show some compassion and sensitivity. After holding his hand through all of his pain and suffering, Atina vowed not to stand by and allow Driscelle to mess him up again.

"Yes, Baby. I'm in the bathroom," she called out to Fabian after hearing him beckon her. She wiped her face and straightened herself up. Grabbing a compact from the counter, she patched up her face, took a deep breath, and went to him.

"I'm not sure this is a good idea," he said as he heard her enter the room.

With her heart racing she asked him, "why, not?"

"I don't know. I'm not sure it's right because I don't know what the girl wants. She may be in some serious trouble."

"She's Abraham's girl, Fabian. Remember, you could never be to her what Abraham is. You heard the girl say that out of her own mouth. She doesn't love you, Fabian. She never has. You've only been her boy toy. If you stop and think about it, she always uses you to do the things that would get her into trouble if she did them herself and got caught. That way there would never be any blood on her hands and Babe, you've always been stupid enough to do whatever she wanted you to do," Atina heard herself say without thinking.

Fabian sat there for a few seconds with rage on his face which scared Atina. She didn't know which of them he was angry at. She stood real still as Fabian began clenching and releasing his fist in an angry yet rhythmic motion. Fabian had never hit her before but she wasn't sure whether or not this would be the first time. He was very sensitive when it came to his feelings for Driscelle. Then something happened that really shocked her, but also brought her joy. Fabian broke down and cried! He summoned her over and held her. He sobbed and sobbed as if to let it all out, but without saying a word. It was as if the spell she had him under had finally broken and for the first time in years, Atina felt like she'd won. She'd finally beaten the wicked witch of the east and Fabian was all hers. As she was rejoicing, Fabian began rubbing her tummy. It was obvious that he had considered their baby and what would happen if he'd gotten involved with Driscelle again. Atina was only a few weeks pregnant. In fact, she wasn't even showing yet. They'd just found out about the baby three weeks before and Fabian nearly jumped out of his shoes with excitement. But they both knew that this baby wasn't his first. They both believed Little Abe was sired by Fabian, not Abraham, and that was the real source of Atina's insecurity. She'd often feared Driscelle using the boy as a way of getting Fabian back when things went sour with Abraham. Until now, things seemed to be going okay between them. It helped that Driscelle didn't keep in touch with them and that she still lived in the uptown apartment. Atina knew Driscelle well and was certain that if she wanted a favor from Fabian, it had something to do with that situation. And she was absolutely right.

Driscelle selected the lingerie she'd wear underneath her clothing to meet Fabian. The ones she chose were "Fabian proof". She laughed wickedly every time she looked at them. "Good-bye, Della", she chanted. "Oh, Fabian, you're still the fool you've always been for me. When will you ever learn? You poor stupid, stupid man," she said as she laughed wickedly again. "And as for you, Mister Abraham, we're going to get it together. I just need to figure out what I want done with your darling Della. Hmmm. What do I want done? I guess I need to see what my dear foolish Fabian is up for doing. Of course, he'll do whatever I tell him to do. If I want you dead, you're going to die. Fabian will kill you and think nothing of it. Anything for his Drissy," she said as she stirred the mashed potatoes she had begun fixing for Little Abe, who had cried himself to sleep in his bedroom.

"Something is just not right about this Patricia," Della said.

"What do you mean?"

"The girl, Driscelle, is crazy. I wouldn't put it past that nut to try to slip poison in his coffee. She's nuts, I tell you. You can see it on her face. She looks like the devil incarnate. At first I thought it was the way she applied her makeup but when I saw her the second time, she didn't have on as much as she did the first time. I'm telling you. That thang is crazy. She's a desperate woman and I wouldn't put anything past her."

"Well, you know what you need to do..."

"I know, I know," she said cutting Patricia off. "I need to pray."

"You guys think I'm just a Jesus freak but I'm telling you, a lot of people are alive today because of someone else's prayers. You might laugh and make fun of me now, but don't let God have to show Himself to you by allowing you to have a real close brush with death in order to get you to pray. I'll bet if you see your life flash before your eyes you won't scoff at this prayer thing, will you?" she said and they both laughed.

"You're right. I know I need to pray more but honestly, if I've never felt the need to pray before, I do now. I'm getting back into it anyway because Abraham is a praying man. I find myself praying more lately than ever before. He seems to be a constant reminder for me."

"You can't get to Heaven on Abraham's ticket, though."

"Don't you start preaching to me or I'm going to hang up in your face. Lately, since Abrie's accident, you've been sounding like your father. It's like you're on a mission to convince everybody that you believe in God. We know, we know," she laughed.

Patricia, who didn't see the humor in it, sat silently for a few seconds on the other end and then said in a very serious tone, "Della, I *am* on a mission. This mission has always been on the inside of me but I had no one to talk to but Abrie. She didn't tease me or make me feel like a fanatic like the rest of you did, and look at our group now. In case you haven't noticed, the 'Five Stair Steps' is now 'The Four Tops'--sorta. In the physical, we're only 'The Three Degrees' and do we know if the other two were ready? I take salvation very seriously and I know you think I'm this way because I grew up in the house with a preacher but nevertheless, God is real and He's no joke. The Bible says we'll be persecuted for our beliefs but, Della, that shouldn't stop us from spreading the Good News. I know I seem to have gone way over the top and I expect the rest of you to eventually stop speaking to me for it, but in the end, He won't have to ask me why I didn't profess Him before man. The bottom line is that it's either you guys or Him, and I chose you before. This time I have to choose Him at whatever cost."

"You're right, Patricia. I know better and I *am* getting back into it. It may seem like Abrie's accident and China's death didn't affect me, but they did. I just don't know how to express it the way you do and I am afraid that people will think I'm strange, too. But like I said, Abraham is leading me back into it."

"From the sounds of it, you and Abraham need to pray together. If this Driscelle is as bad as you think she is, who knows what she'll do? The only protection we have is God but unfortunately, not enough people recognize that."

"He's very concerned. In fact, I think he's kinda scared of her---and rightfully so."

"You may not want to hear this but if he truly trusted the God to whom he prays, he wouldn't have to be afraid of a possessed woman like that. But on the other hand, if he's truly afraid, you both need to be praying. What do you think he's afraid of exactly?"

"I think it's a combination of things, but I really don't want to get into that now. It's getting late and I still have a couple more calls to make."

"Speaking of which, have you heard from Nancy?"

"I sure have. She's called me a few times and I haven't been able to get back to her yet. She's one of the calls I have to make. She called me the other day to tell me something about Ross and Marlena both showing up to her house, but I didn't have time to talk to her. I was going to meet Abraham for breakfast and my mind was on figuring out what he'd possibly have to talk to me about that couldn't wait until the afternoon at least. Anyway, let me go because I'm going to try to catch her before she leaves work."

"Okay. I need to finish these files on my desk before I go home today anyway, so I'll talk to you later," she said before hanging up.

As Della went to call Nancy, she got a page and was told that Abraham was on the phone. She picked up and found out he'd taken the paternity test and would have to wait for the results. She was quite surprised that he'd had it done so quickly but was a little puzzled as to how he was able to get Little Abe to the lab. As it turned out, he'd convinced Driscelle to let him take his son out so they could spend some time together, and since she was planning to go out later on, it worked out for her. Abraham laughed as he wondered what would happen when Little Abe let Driscelle know that he'd gotten a "shot". He kept saying, "Daddy, I got a shot but it didn't hurt." Surprisingly, Little Abe wasn't scared of the needle. Abraham and Della joked at the thought that he could be seeing needles regularly around Driscelle, but they both knew that shooting up was not one of her many flaws.

Abraham did feel badly about taking the boy under those circumstances, even though consent was really not a problem. There had been a previous court order for a paternity test, which was never followed through. His mother, who was very influential in the community because of a successful political career, had pulled some strings and taken care of all of the paperwork. Driscelle had sweet talked him into not taking the test but didn't realize that the paperwork was still on file and valid.

"Daddy, Daddy," Little Abe was screaming. "Look!" He was pointing at different animals at the Ravenwood Zoo. Abraham had taken his son there because it was one of his favorite places to go. Little Abe was so excited that he let go of Abraham's hand, hugged him around the leg and said, "I love you, Daddy, and I love the zoo."

"I love you, too, Buddy," he said as he freed his leg from Little Abe's grip and picked him up to hug and kiss him. Instantly, Abraham felt badly about the test and wished he hadn't done it. For the next few hours at the zoo, he was slightly distracted as he tried to decide if he should even find out the results of the test. Would it change the way he felt about his little boy? Wouldn't he love Little Abe the same and vice versa? How would he break the news to his son? He knew that if Driscelle found out about how he really felt, she would use it against him. She would do something insensitive and crazy like blurting out to the little boy, "that's not your daddy so stop calling him that. He doesn't care about you. That's why he had the test done behind my back." And there was no doubt she'd bring Della into the picture. She'd probably say something like, "he loved you until he met that *#@#*. She obviously means more to him than you do and he chose her because he's not smart enough to know that he can love two people."

"Daddy, can I? Please, Daddy?" Little Abe was pleading as Abraham came back to reality.

"Can you what, man?"

"Can I have a big candy? One of those pink ones."

"You mean cotton candy, and yes, you may," Abraham answered as they walked over to buy one. They shared it because it was too big for Little Abe to eat by himself. After he'd eaten what he did, his face was a sticky mess. That to Abraham was a Kodak moment. His sadness deepened. He realized, more than ever before, that he really did love his son and would do anything for him. He had to question himself about the importance of the test results. Would it really matter? "What have I gotten myself into?" he mumbled to himself. By this time he was wiping Little Abe's face with a wet paper towel. After grimacing with each wipe, Little Abe looked at him and smiled. Abraham kissed him, lifted him up to his chest and swung him back and forth. "I love you, Little Man. You are my life."

TWENTY-FIVE

"So, I see you made it," Driscelle said as she looked up at Fabian.

"Actually, I did. I'm sure you're not surprised."

"No, I'm really not. I knew you wouldn't let me down. You never have," she said seductively.

"I wish I could say the same."

"Oh, my. A little salty, are we? I apologized for what happened, Babe."

"Babe? Okay, Driscelle. What do you want?"

"Don't you want it, too?"

"It depends on what it is."

"Don't you know?"

"Drissy, I know you better than you think. I know you didn't call me down here because you want to have sex. I know better than that. Sex with you was always payment for something, so what is it?"

"You're awfully pushy tonight. Don't you want to spend some time together before we get down to business?" she asked as she put his hands on her breast.

"Not really. I have to know what I'm getting myself into first. So what is it? Are you in some kind of trouble?" he asked as he removed his hands.

"Fabian, you're more handsome than I remember," she said stroking his goatee. "I like the hair on your face. It brings out your masculinity."

For the first time, Fabian felt completely turned off by Driscelle. More than turned off, he was disgusted. Her words and actions made him feel cheap. She was way too forward and there was a desperation about her that was not becoming. Fabian realized he just needed closure, and he got it. After all these years, he thought he still loved her but he didn't. She lacked the softness of Atina. As he realized he didn't love Driscelle, he realized he loved Atina more than he thought. It was Tine who had his heart. She sort of blind-sided him. Her love crept up on him and had to have been there far longer than he previously thought. Driving to Farlane's, he thought he would live to regret his decision to go but he actually appreciated it.

In the car, Atina was praying hard, "please God. Please don't let her take my husband from me. Help him to see that what we have is special. Put the baby on his mind and please don't let him walk out on us. God, you gave this family to me. Please, God, please don't take it away." Atina prayed harder than she had in years and was hoping against hope that if there was a God up there, He'd hear her.

"Are you listening to me Fabian?"

"Actually, Driscelle, I'm not. I don't even know why I came down here."

"What?" She was absolutely astonished.

"I said I don't know why I came down here. As a matter of fact, I do know why. I came down here to see if I still had feelings for you but I realize that I don't. You don't move me the way you used to Drissy. You hurt me more than anyone else in life and I have been through a lot. You're throwing yourself at me like some kind of cheap whore and it is really turning me off."

"Oh, really. I'll bet you won't be turned off after seeing this," she said as she went to unbutton her blouse. He stopped her by grabbing her hands and laughing. That made her angry.

"Time has passed and things have changed, Drissy, but I guess uptown, not much has changed."

"What's that supposed to mean?" she hissed.

"Come with me. I want to show you something."

Atina's heart pounded as she looked out the deeply tinted windows and saw them coming toward her. She just knew they were coming to invite her out of the car or to make her sit in the backseat so Driscelle could sit in the front. When they got close enough, Fabian tapped on her window and said to Driscelle, "I'd like you to meet my wife and child."

As if on cue, Atina rolled the window down and said, "Hello, Driscelle."

If Driscelle could have, she would have spit nails. "Hello Atina. So where's the wife and child?" she asked with clinched teeth, "because I know you didn't get that desperate."

"Oh, no you didn't," Atina said and laughed. She was elated at the fact that he'd brought Driscelle over and introduced her as his wife.

"Oh, no *you* didn't. I can't believe this. This has to be a joke. What, Atina, you couldn't find your own so you had to have mine?"

"Yours?" Atina and Fabian asked at the same time.

"When did he become yours?" Atina asked. "You were the fool who let him go and what happened to Abraham, the boy wonder? Is he tired of your old, ugly ways, too?"

At that second, Driscelle remembered what her mission was. Her anger was boosted by a surge of desperation and much to everyone's surprise, she hauled off and slapped Fabian so hard it sounded like a clap. As Fabian grabbed his face, Atina snatched the door open. Fabian stood in front of her and between the two of them as a bunch of harsh words, finger pointing and neck rolling took place. He was finally able to get Atina back in the car and close the door before he turned to her and said, "if my girl weren't pregnant, I'd let her beat you down. Maybe we'll see you in a few months." At that, he got in on the driver's side, started up the car and sped off. Driscelle was fighting mad by this point and stood in the parking lot screaming, snorting, ranting and raving like a rabid animal. She was so angry she broke down crying. Still screaming, not caring who was watching, she stormed to her car and took off.

"So, how's your face?"

"How do you think my face is?" Fabian chuckled. "That sucker hurts right about now. That girl packs a powerful punch but it was worth it. Did you see the look on her face when I said 'wife'? That girl about jumped out of her skin."

"Yea, I about jumped out of mine when she slapped you."

"Baby, you would have fought for me?"

"That's a dumb question. Let's go get something to eat. We're hungry," she said as she rubbed her belly. Fabian reached over to rub it with her. The two of them smiled.

"By the way, what did she want?" Atina asked.

"You know, I really don't know. We never got that far. But it's really not important, is it? Baby, tonight I realized that the most important thing in the world to me is you."

"Thank You, God," she murmured to herself. "Thank You." She grabbed his hand and caressed it until they got to one of their favorite fast food places.

Driscelle was so angry her vision was blurred. She pulled into her parking space, almost hitting the curb. Slamming the door as she got out, she shouted obscenities all the way to her door. After entering, she frantically paced the floor for most of the night, forgetting to pick up Little Abe as she'd promised.

Across town, Abraham was hoping she'd call and ask him to let Little Abe spend the night. She often did that as she went out on her escapades, so he expected his son to have to spend the night. The zoo trip wore Little Abe out to the point of him falling asleep in his dinner plate. Abraham picked him up and cleaned him up as best he could. Little Abe wasn't in the most cooperative of moods because he just wanted to sleep. Abraham had powdered him down, slipped his pajamas on him and laid him in his bed. Then he cleaned himself up and returned to Little Abe's room. He held his son, staring at him until he drifted off to sleep. Driscelle never bothered to call but that didn't bug Abraham at all. As far as he was concerned, she didn't ever have to show up. The day had been long for him as he reflected back on his decision to get the paternity test. He was sorry he did.

Driscelle had decided to pour herself a drink. For the first time in years, she felt alone. Della had Abraham and Atina had Fabian. For the last five years, she'd had them both. She couldn't face the possibility of having no one, so one drink turned into enough for her to see oblivion. She passed out on the couch. Anyone coming in would have seen the family resemblance. She had turned into what she never wanted to be: her mother.

Della wondered how the day went for "Big Abe and Little Abe." She'd hoped they'd bond and Abraham would rethink what he was doing, but then asked herself whether or not it was too late for him to think it over. The paternity test had been done but she didn't see what good it would do. A part of her knew he needed to know, but the other side of her said it wouldn't be worth it to leave the boy fatherless. It would definitely change the relationship between them, but the truth really needed to come out--no matter how damaging. Better now than later, she convinced herself. She knew she'd need to be there for him regardless of the findings. She really felt for the little boy. He had a crazy mother and now the possibility of losing his daddy existed. "Why, Abraham? Why, now?"

She remembered her conversation with Patricia and decided that now was the time to pray, but she didn't know what to ask for, or if God would even hear her.

It had been such a long time since she'd spoken to Him from the heart, but she did it anyway. "Dear God. I guess that's how I'm supposed to start this. I know it's been a long time and I probably have my nerves trying to talk to you now but this one isn't about me. It's been a long time since *we've* talked, but Abraham talks to you daily. God, You know what he needs, but I don't. I don't even know what to pray for because I don't know what's best, but You do and Abraham knows You do. Please give him the right answer and help him to deal with whatever it is. I guess that's all. Amen. I hope you heard that, God. A little boy's life is at stake here. Please help Little Abe. He didn't ask for any of this. Amen."

TWENTY-SIX

Ross SAT IN HIS APARTMENT contemplating whether or not to call Marlena. He really didn't know what he wanted to say to her. He didn't miss her, so that wouldn't have been a good reason to call. For that matter, he didn't love her either, so the idea to call her must have come from some way out place in his mind. He didn't know why he even entertained it, but there was an urging deep down on the inside of him to give her a call. He picked up the receiver several times before deciding that he just wasn't ready to talk. The thought ran through his mind that it was now or never. Ross was reminded of the fact that he was a major procrastinator and because of it, things in his life didn't get done. He wouldn't have this problem had he not waited for the "right time" with Bianca. She deserved more from him than what she'd gotten. Bianca wanted to get married and have children and Ross denied her that--or did he? Maybe it wasn't meant for her to give birth for had she done so, her children would have been left without a mother. Or maybe had she given birth, she wouldn't have developed breast cancer.

"There's so much noise in my head at times," he said aloud. "I just want it all to go away and leave me alone." But the noise wouldn't stop. He was bombarded with a bunch of "what-ifs" and "maybe-you-should-haves" that were driving him to want to take a drink even though he wasn't a drinker. After about forty-five minutes, he conceded.

"Hello," a voice cracked from the other end.

"Marlena?"

"Ross?"

"Yes, it's me. Uh, I'm going to visit Abrie today but I want to go early. So if you have something else to do, I'll be there."

"Thanks, but I need to be there for her, too. How have you been?"

"I'm fine. How about you?"

"I'm doing okay," she said with a cracking in her voice he'd never heard before.

"Lena, I know we need to talk, but I'm just not ready yet," he said as if asking her permission to talk later.

"Then why did you call, Ross?"

"I'm not sure. I felt this urging inside to do so, so I did, if you want to know the truth."

"The truth is always nice. The truth in like who Bianca is, but I already know now. Why didn't you ever tell me?"

After a long pause, "Who told you about Bianca?"

"Does it matter? The one who should have told me about her neglected to do so, so what's the point?"

"The point is," Ross began angrily, "that you shouldn't be snooping around in my business. Who have you been talking to about her?"

"Ross, *you* should have told me about her. How could you keep something like that a secret? You must have been suffering greatly," she said showing some compassion that Ross didn't trust.

Relenting some, he said, "I have, but this is not the time or the place to talk about it. I have some things to do before heading over to the rehab center. I'll see you there."

"Ross, when will be the right time to talk about it? You obviously couldn't find the right time in more than ten years. How much time do you need?"

"Marlena, I could have told you, but you were too busy with your preoccupation with Reggie. You didn't want to hear *from* me or *about* me in the more than ten years we were together. Why do you care now?"

"*Were* together?"

"Yes, Lane. *Were* together."

"Ross, what are you saying?"

"I'm saying that I have some things to do and if you're at the center later, I'll see you then."

Before she could respond, he hung up. Marlena was devastated. She had a strong feeling that Ross was not going to want to work things out, but that was just not like him. What had Abrie's accident done to him? It was almost as if something in him died or maybe he died as a whole. He was so incredibly cold when it came to her and it was downright hard for her to handle. She didn't know he had it in him to be this way, but it seems there were lots of things about Ross that she wasn't aware of.

After talking to Ross' brother, Freddie, she learned about many things that he'd kept hidden. It seemed that good old Ross had a whole past that she'd never heard about. According to Freddie, Ross had bought some land in South Carolina to build a house for Bianca before she'd fallen ill. He had a couple of ranches with horses, cows and other livestock. He owned condominiums in California and apartment complexes in Denver, Colorado. He owned several companies that she'd had no knowledge of and had made some major investments that proved very lucrative for him. The place where he reported to work on Monday through Friday was doing much better than she'd ever imagined, but it took his brother to reveal all of that to her. But the fact of the matter was that Ross *had* tried to talk to her--on more than one occasion. That wasn't the problem. The problem was that Marlena never wanted to hear about it. But Abrie knew. She always listened when Ross told stories about his life. That's one of the many reasons they were so close. She enjoyed his stories about Bianca, the horses, the ranches, the livestock, the condos, the apartment complexes and the businesses. She also enjoyed hearing Ross' accounts of the encounters he'd had with the people from the different regions of the United States and abroad. Another thing Marlena didn't know was that Abrie was the sole beneficiary of most of what Ross owned. He'd decided long ago that she was the closest he'd ever get to having a daughter and he was just fine with that. He loved her more than life itself because she allowed him to be who he was. No frills, no thrills. Just Ross. She wasn't impressed by the money or the status and there was nothing phony about her love for him. He had learned early in life that if people know who you are or what you have, you never get to see them for who or what they really are. They will always wear their Sunday best for you and put smiles on while you're right in front of them, but jealousy, envy or insecurity eats them alive on the inside and before you know it, they hate you. They decide that you think you're better than they are and that you think little of them; especially when you're trying to help them. People, by nature, unless they have the Spirit of God, are ruthless, envious crabs in a barrel, and Ross had had his share of dealings in that arena. He'd come close to losing his business to a best friend gone bad. That was one of the main reasons he became so low key about his life. In his younger years, he made the mistake that many people with good ideas or fortune make--he shared it with people who he'd considered close to him. The problem with that is that everyone who should be happy for you isn't necessarily thrilled when things take a turn in your favor. In Ross' case, Melvin, a childhood friend, decided that Ross didn't need to be rich all by himself. What he didn't understand was that Ross felt the same way and had planned all along to take Melvin straight to the top with him. Melvin's problem was lack. He lacked faith, confidence, diligence, and patience, which are the main ingredients for success. Melvin wanted to get rich quick and because of that, he spent every dime he got his fingers on. He tried to make a dollar out of fifteen cents whereas Ross understood the harvesting process. Ross knew to plant the seed, cultivate it, watch it grow and, when it was time, to reap the harvest of his crops. They'd made a few thousand dollars on one of Ross' business ideas and Melvin blew his as he flossed for his friends and family members. Ross, on the other hand, invested his. He tried to get Melvin to do the same but he wouldn't hear of it. Whenever there was a good return on an investment, Melvin would buy cars, houses, clothes, jewelry, etc. Ross' life didn't appear to change at all. He wore the same clothing he wore before the returns and drove the same cars. It was obvious that he had a plan. When the golden opportunity presented itself, Ross tried to convince Melvin to invest his share of the profits. The investment goal was too long term for Melvin. He scoffed at Ross and told him that he was crazy for putting all of his "eggs in one basket." But Ross knew it was a sure fire thing. The return on the investment came a lot sooner than even Ross expected but by this time, Melvin was nearly broke. From the goodness of his heart, mixed with way too much sympathy, Ross shared his cut with his friend. But this time, the share wasn't monetary. Ross invested in some business machines and built a successful business. He made Melvin a partner. The business proved extremely lucrative and in his excitement, Ross shared everything with Melvin. Before long, the business started booming and expansion was necessary. Melvin started hiring family members and friends and began pilfering from the business. He did everything from taking money from the safe to cheating on the taxes. He even tried to sell one of the businesses right from under Ross' nose. Melvin had convinced himself that Ross didn't need it and wouldn't miss it anyway. When it was all said and done, Melvin spat foul words at Ross, accusing him of insulting his integrity with the "hand-outs" he was trying to give him. He accused Ross of changing after getting his money and, instead of trusting him as a real friend would, he kept it away from him and tried to get him to be his "show-boy." Ross learned the painful lesson that business and pleasure don't mix, and that friends don't always make the best business partners-- especially if they were irresponsible from the beginning. Or as he would tell Abrie, "you can't make stallions out of serpents, no matter how hard you try or how thick your blinders are. Serpents are snakes and will never, ever be prize winning horses no matter how much you try to disguise them with your denial, ignorance and/ or fear of being alone."

Melvin was another part of his past that his wife knew nothing about, but it wasn't because he never tried to tell her. In his apartment, Ross had gone over and over in his mind the many things he'd wanted to tell her over the years that she'd never had time to hear about. Many a night, he cried himself to sleep out of frustration. He couldn't believe he'd been such a fool all these years, but because of the family therapy at the rehab center, he was realizing that it was all due to his grief. He'd convinced himself all these years that none of it mattered but in all actuality, Ross was suffering from depression. He covered it up well, but any trained mental health professional would have seen it right away. All of the signs and symptoms were there. The fact that he'd settled for a relationship that wasn't meeting his needs showed the guilt he felt for not marrying Bianca.

It was also obvious that he was punishing himself for it, and that, in his mind, the punishment could never be harsh enough. The fact that he'd taken on Reggie Lofton's children and played the role of mother and father showed him trying to compensate for having denied Bianca the children she wanted. The fact that he never forgave himself for not having been there for his beloved the way he felt he should have, could have explained why he'd taken so much abuse and neglect from Marlena for so long.

Marlena took out on Ross all the anger she felt for Reggie, so she was finding out in her sessions with her therapist. On this particular day, she was crying her eyes out for Ross and screaming at Reggie. For the first time in more than a decade, she admitted that she was really angry at Reggie for having been so hardheaded. She was angry at him for putting her through this. If only he had listened. Why did he have to be so stubborn? At one point in the session, she screamed, "This is good for you, Reggie Lofton. *You* got what *you* deserved but did *we* deserve this? We didn't go out and buy that stupid motorcycle for you. I tried to tell you to stay away but you wouldn't listen and now all of us have to suffer. I hope you're happy. You're the only one who got what you wanted. Did you really want to get away from me that badly? Reggieeeee...Reggieeeee... she wailed as she slid from her seat onto the floor. The therapist thought it best to end the session at that point, of course allowing her some regroup time before she left the office.

By this time, Ross had made it to his office and was silently grieving for Bianca. He was due there for an appointment but his client didn't show up. "Surprise, surprise," he thought to himself aloud as he began to speak to Bianca in a low whisper. "Baby, I am so sorry. Why couldn't I have been there for you? You didn't ask for much, Bee, but I was so selfish. All I could think about was Ross and what Ross wanted, but Bee, I was doing it for you, too. I just wanted you to have the best of everything. I didn't want to marry you and have both of us struggle to make ends meet. Bee, I wanted you to live a life of luxury. That's what you deserved. I love you, Bee. I'll always love you. Will you ever forgive me for not being there for you? I need that from you, Bee. I need you to forgive me." At that moment, Ross felt something lift from him that left him a sense of peace and a smile on his face as he leaned back in his chair. Tears spilled from his closed eyes as he seemingly received Bianca's forgiveness and embrace. For the first time in more than ten years, Ross felt a deep sense of peace and the guilt he carried was not heavy on his chest. "Thank you. Thank you so much for understanding, Bee. I knew you would." Ross' eyes opened abruptly as he realized where he was and that he was by himself. He was almost afraid to look behind him for what he might find. He was left startled. If felt to him as if Bianca were in the room with him. He had never experienced that feeling before but he'd never asked for forgiveness, either. He thought for sure he was losing his mind.

TWENTY-SEVEN

DRISCELLE SHOWED UP AT ABRAHAM'S house to pick up
Little Abe only to find a note taped to the door saying
they'd gone out to breakfast and would be back shortly.
She was twelve hours late, which Abraham expected.
When she found the note, her mind began running
away with her. Immediately, Della came to mind and
before long, she'd convinced herself that Abraham had
taken the two of them out so they could get to know
each other better. The thought of "that woman" cozying
up to her son made her want to spit nails. She paced for
a few minutes before getting into her car, where she sat
for about three minutes before returning and deciding
to go to a back window to try to pry it open. With
nothing available to assist her, she walked back around
to the front. By the time Abraham had driven up, he
could tell that she was trying to break in the front door.
Irritated, he got out of the car and asked her what she
was doing. Hysterically, she began accusing him of
having tried to brainwash her son and turn him against
her by plotting to make Della number one in his life.

She swore before him that "that woman" would never have the opportunity to raise her son. Before he knew it, Abraham had responded to her by saying, "Oh, so *you* don't want to do it and you don't want *anyone else* to raise him either, huh?" There was dead silence for a few long seconds before he apologized. He really meant it but he didn't want to make a scene in front of the child. Although he was cognizant of the fact that the four year old was present, she didn't seem to care. She ranted and raved about Della having touched her son and that she'd need to bathe him to get her scent off him. He tried to explain to her that the two of them had dined alone but she wouldn't hear it.

"What's really going on, Driscelle?" he asked. "What is it you really want from me and why must there always be drama whenever you come around?"

Much to his surprise, she answered, "I want you, Abraham. I want us to be a family like we were meant to be."

Abraham looked at her with absolute disgust, and then walked around to the passenger side of his car to let his boy out. Little Abe always seemed to handle his mother's outbursts like a champ. He'd seen so many of them that he was actually used to it. He really didn't expect anything different from her, though they seemed to make him very sad.

"We need to talk," he said as he was letting Little Abe into the house. "I am going to put in his favorite movie and we can go into the kitchen to talk, provided you don't get loud. If you get loud and indignant, I will end the conversation and invite you to leave. If you refuse, I will call the police, and I mean it, Driscelle.

Do I make myself clear? No outbursts and no drama," he demanded. "Deal?"

"Deal," she said as she smiled, obviously thinking they were going to discuss her proposal.

After getting Little Abe squared away, he invited her into the kitchen and asked her if she wanted anything to eat or drink. In anticipation of the good news, she declined.

"Driscelle, how could you even suggest such a thing after all that's happened?"

"It's that woman, isn't it? It's because of her that you don't..."

Abraham threw his hand up in a gesture that halted Driscelle in her tracks. He dropped his head for a few seconds, in an effort to collect himself. When he did, he began to speak.

"You know things were over between us long before Della. You're always looking for someone or something to blame. Look at you. Look at the way you carry on. What man in his right mind would want to be with a woman who is always screaming, accusing, nagging and creating scenes whenever he tries to talk to her?"

"I'm not creating a scene now, am I?"

"Not yet, but I'm sure it's coming."

"I told you I wasn't going to get loud. Give me a chance, Baby. Let me show you that I can behave."

"How could you even think we could be a family? I can't deal with your behavior. I can't stand the way you act. It's embarrassing. You have destroyed too much of my life. I couldn't go back to that style of living if I wanted to."

"But I've changed, Abe. You know I have..."

"No you haven't," he interrupted. "You've actually gotten worse, and besides, I could never take you home to my mother."

"Okay, Momma's boy. What does she have to do with this? You know that's why things didn't work the first time. Why can't we just leave her out of our lives?"

"How dare you accuse my mother of being the reason for us not being together? We can't be together because we are from two different sides of the tracks, Driscelle and you know it. You and I are like dirty oil and clean water..."

"Oh but Miss Della is just right for you I guess. What does she have that I don't have?"

"Is that a rhetorical question or just a plain old stupid one?"

"It's not a stupid question. I really want to know what she has that I don't have..."

"Try class, Driscelle."

"What are you trying to say? Are you saying that I have no class?"

"And you're surprised? Look at the things you do. You...," he stopped himself and began rubbing his temples. "I'm not going to let you do this to me today. There's something else I need to discuss with you but I need your word that you won't nut up. Can you just give me that? If you get loud, the conversation is over and you'll have to leave, okay. Do I have your word?"

"Word," she said sarcastically.

After a long sigh, he blurted it out, "I took Little Abe down and had the paternity test done."

"You did what?" she said in a louder than normal voice, and as if she didn't already know.

"If there's going to be drama, we can end this conversation now," he said.

"I can't believe you did this behind my back. What in the..."

"Do you need to leave? If we're going to finish this conversation, you're going to have to settle down."

The fear in her was obvious. She started fidgeting and drumming her fingers on the dining room table. "No, I don't need to leave, but I need to know why you felt the need to do this behind my back."

"For starters, there are the obvious reasons, and I didn't do it behind your back. I told you that it needed to be done, so technically, I didn't do it behind your back. I just did it sooner than you thought I would. The opportunity was there so I took full advantage of it. What's so wrong with that? We were going to do it anyway."

"I know, but you could have waited until I was ready."

"The boy is four years old. How much more time did you need? But that's beside the point..."

"Beside the point. You took my son--our son--to a hospital and had blood drawn from him and..."

"I don't know if I want to know the results of the test."

"What?" she asked surprised.

"I said I don't know if I want to know."

"This might sound like a stupid question," she said with some relief, "but what was the point in having the test done?"

"At the time, I wanted to know. After spending time with him today, I realize that he's my son and nothing is going to change that. The only person who really knows is God and probably you, but that's neither here nor there. I think this is something I'd rather leave alone. I love Little Abe and nothing is going to change that, but I want you to know one thing."

"And what might that be?"

"The next time you try something stupid, the envelope is coming open."

"What envelope?"

"The one with the test results in it. You need to know that I will cut you off if they show that I'm not the boy's father. I will never cut him off, but *you* will go without. Are we clear on this? Driscelle, I am tired of playing this game with you. I'm tired of you messing around in my life, and I hate that it's come to this but something has got to change and, unless you want to go back to living in the hood, I suggest you start acting like you belong in the division you're living in right now. Understood?"

"Understood," she said knowing that he had the upper hand. At that, he went into the living room to spend some more time with Little Abe and invited her to stay for a few minutes if she'd like. She accepted and sat down on an easy chair not far from the Abes, who were wrestling around on the ground by the time she got there. She needed a few minutes to regroup. As she sat, the images from last night rolled around in her mind. The thought of getting rid of Della took a back seat as she realized she'd been given some time. If she'd never seen a serious Abraham before, she'd seen it this day. Somehow she knew he meant business. There was something very different about him and he was right. She didn't want to move back to her old hood, especially with Atina and Fabian being married. *Married*. She couldn't believe it. Atina had stolen her back up and once again she found herself feeling alone. More alone than ever before. As a matter of fact, she was vulnerable. Very, very vulnerable, and this feeling was not a new one for her. Vulnerability is what made her do what she had done in the first place. Having a substance abuser for a mother leaves you feeling vulnerable a lot and having grown up feeling alone, scared, ashamed, and lonely all the time made her vow that as an adult she would never, ever be left to fend for herself again. The only problem was that she went about establishing her security in a wrong way. A very wrong way.

TWENTY-EIGHT

As NANCY WAS DRIVING UP the turnpike, she had a nasty thought about all of her too busy friends who no longer had time for her. In reality, she was only talking about Della. One of Nancy's problems was that she was spoiled and expected everyone to be at her beck and call. Of course, this rule didn't work both ways. It was a part of her perfectionism and although she would have never admitted it, she was terribly jealous of Della's relationship with Abraham. She mumbled to herself about her "friends" for most of the ride to her parent's house, where she'd decided to retreat for a few days. She didn't bother to call anyone because she figured they needed to miss her. This would show them that she was not to be ignored or neglected. It had been far too long since she'd visited her parents and was due for a trip home anyway. Both her parents were excited about her coming, but she felt a little bit awkward. In fact, she felt downright guilty. After so many years of having accused her father of something she now knew he would have never done, she almost felt unworthy of setting foot on his premises. She almost felt, though, a need to make amends, and the biggest step in doing that had to be taken where it all began. The drive wasn't too long or too bad and it gave her the opportunity to wind down from her own life and the things that had happened in it in the last few months. She'd, in essence, lost two of her best friends. She wondered how Abrie was doing because she hadn't gone to see her in months. She'd heard she was making progress but hadn't seen it herself. If asked why, she wouldn't have had an answer. Was it that she needed time to figure it all out, or was it that she didn't really know what to say or do when she got there? She didn't feel comfortable visiting the rehabilitation center and she didn't know how she'd feel about visiting her at home, since her parents were acting so strangely. She never did figure out what their visits were all about. Why did Marlena accuse her of having entertained Ross in her home? Did Marlena really know how she felt about Ross and if so, how long had she known? And Ross? Why did he show up at her house and what did he really want? Do you suppose it was a...? No way! It couldn't have been. Ross was too classy for that, but what if it was? Curious, her mind started to spin out of control. What if it was? (She began to feel flattered.) It could have been, but we won't even get into that Ross, because that is not going to happen--not here, not with me.

Her father greeted her as she pulled into the driveway. He had been outside mowing the lawn and saw her car when she rounded the corner. He was very glad to see her. He helped her unload her vehicle and carry her belongings inside the house where she was greeted by her very excited and cheerful mother. Her parents were very happy people; well, they were usually happy people. The deacon board at the church had them running in circles. Not much had changed since before her father's visit, but at least things hadn't gotten worse. Nancy and her parents spent time together that evening watching old movies, eating dinner and after dinner snacks. Her parents love for each other, along with their vim and vigor, reminded her of people a lot younger than they were. She delighted to see the way they touched each other while sneaking passionate glances. Nancy had mixed feelings about it, though. She loved the fact that her parents were still very much in love after so many years of marriage. She felt awful having thought her father would violate such a covenant, and she was sure her mother knew what her problem had been all these years. Their happiness saddened her because it reminded her that she hadn't found anyone to share her life with, and the only man she'd ever really cared for had a wife and a family, as well as other obligations. It also reminded her that she had been willing to compromise her values and settle for less. She was willing to settle for being the other woman--a fate worse than death to her. Ross would have never given her the attention her dad gave to her mother. For that matter, most men weren't as attentive to their wives as her dad was to her mother. Her parents had done it right, though. They waited on God, which seems endless to most people. No sooner than the thought ran through her mind, her mother began to speak about the things she'd had to go through as God prepared her to be a wife and her husband to be a husband.

Nancy's mother was not stupid. She could read the look on Nancy's face and that was probably because she'd seen it on the faces of so many others who'd seen the interaction between the two of them. Their love was genuine. It was the kind that had to have been sent from up above. The kind everybody wanted, but no one was willing to wait for because it took too long. Love from above takes a very long time to cultivate and people these days are way too needy to wait. The Bible says that those who wait up on the Lord shall mount up with wings like eagles, but most people settle for sparrow-like living because it's quicker, though not necessarily easier. It's like a band-aid on an open wound because you get into the relationship knowing it's not going to work, but you try everything you can to keep it together. Then when you become saturated, you realize your system isn't really working and all you can do is put on a new band-aid. The point is that you have to keep changing the band-aid and even if the wound closes up, it's going to leave an ugly scar. Why don't people see that if they'd just go to the Doctor in the first place, the wound would be properly tended to and, though it may take longer, the wound would have a chance to heal completely? The problem is that no one has time to see the Doctor anymore. We just patch things up ourselves. Go figure.

"Yea, Nance," her dad said as she was finishing her thoughts, "it wasn't easy by any stretch of the imagination but it was certainly worth it."

"Guys, this is not going to turn into one of those 'Nancy-when-are-you-going-to-get-married' sessions, is it? Because if it is, I'm going to bed."

"No, darling," her mother said. "It's actually one of those 'Gee-Nancy-I'm-glad-to-see-you're-waiting-take-your-time-and-do-it-right' sessions." Everyone laughed.

"That's the good news. I'm not up for the 'why-aren't-you-married' questionnaire that I get from most people. As you know, good men are hard to find."

"And being a good woman takes proper care, training and maintenance," her mother said, surprising her.

"The trick to marriage is not finding the right person. It's being made right for each other. Everyone is looking for the perfect mate but there's no such thing. God doesn't make people perfect. He forgives them for their sins, but even that doesn't make them perfect. What He does is perfect love between two people as they come together as one. That in a nutshell is what the whole process of marriage is all about," her dad chimed in. "I'm doing a seminar on marriage and I'm learning a lot. I can remember what I felt as I was going through this process with your mother. I was scared. I was scared she wouldn't be right for me and I was scared I wouldn't be right for her. I thought I was going to find out things about her that would totally turn me off and that she would find out things about me that would totally turn her off. I feared not being able to do for her what she needed to have done and that she wouldn't be able to satisfy my needs for a lifetime. Fortunately for us, God knew what we both needed and prepared us to be all that for each other. Even today, we are not perfect people but we are perfect in the love we have for God and for one another. It's all about relationship and knowing your role in that relationship--which cannot be defined by other people, contrary to popular belief. In different belief systems and religions, it is taught that there is a one-size-fits-all relationship with God, but how can that be if the body of Christ has several different members, which don't all have the same function? It's kind of like teaching the body of Christ to all function as a foot or as a hand or an eye. If we're all taught the same thing, most of us are going to feel awkward and out of place. That's why the body of Christ is so rebellious. They don't know their places in the body and when they go to the churches for training, they are being taught to be something they're not. The saddest part is that they end up angry at God because of it."

Nancy found herself wanting to hear more. She had never heard it explained like this before and it actually made a lot of sense. She'd always liked her father's teachings, even as a teenager, but had missed so much because of their situation. What made his teachings different was that he taught for the right reasons: because he loved God and wanted others to be able to love Him, too. "Go on, Dad. Finish. I think I want to hear this one."

"Well, many misunderstand what marriage really is. Marriage is a spiritual connection between God and two people, and it is a type of ministry. Ministry means service, so when the Bible talks about submitting and "withholding not affection" from your mate, it's all a part of your service to God, to each other, and to those who are learning about marriage from watching you. In your service to your mate, you have the assigned duty of being the part of the "one flesh" that the other isn't. When "the two flesh become one", only one of you needs to be the hearing and the other's responsibility is to see, for example. If you could come together as one body literally, why would you need four ears or four eyes? One of you sees what God is leading you to do and the other hears it, but you both learn what is expected of you in the marriage. You come together like grooves and protrusions that are made to fit together perfectly. No *human being* can tell you how to make your marriage work, or what to do exactly—unless that's his job in the Kingdom. In marriage, there absolutely needs to be communication with God, as one sees and the other hears. It's really not that complicated."

"Well, Reverend, you've certainly made a believer out of me. When I decide to do it, I'll make sure we get counseling from you. On that note, I think I am going to retire for the evening." And she did.

Her parents, however, stayed up to discuss what they'd been talking about and her reaction to it. They knew something was wrong and they knew what to do. Both of them sensed the emptiness in their daughter and were deeply saddened by it. Together they prayed for wisdom and understanding for her. They also prayed to God that He'd supply her every need according to His riches in glory. Although they knew there'd be a struggle, they knew she would be okay. The victory would be hers in the end. Amen.

TWENTY-NINE

"HI, THIS IS NANCY. LEAVE a message at the beep and I'll return your call as soon as I can."

"Hey, Nance. It's Della. If you're there, pick up the phone. Well, I guess you're not there so call me when you get in. You know the number."

I wonder where she is, Della thought as she hung up the phone. She'd left three messages in the last couple of days and none of them had been returned. "That's not like Nancy," Della thought aloud. "She must have gone out of town, but why didn't she tell anyone? Oh, well. I'll get in touch with her eventually. You can run, Nance, but you can't hide-owwwww!" She screamed. She looked down at her hand and saw a strange insect injecting her with its venom. She shook it off and screamed, "What is that?" Not thinking much more of it than the shock of having been stung, she swatted it, scooped it up and threw it into the garbage can. "There are so many strange critters running around this stupid office. Owww that hurt." Della ignored the painful, tingling sensation as best she could and continued toward the completion of the project she'd come in that morning to work on. Feeling a little light headed, she ended up going home immediately after putting on the finishing touches.

Upon returning home and checking her messages, she returned Abraham's call to find out that he'd been missing her and just wanted to hear her voice. He told her what had happened with Driscelle and that he'd gotten the feeling that she was really going to back off. They laughed and joked about the situation for a few minutes and went on to other topics of conversation. Before the phone call ended, Abraham told her of his shift change and asked if he could drop by a little later. Of course Della agreed to the visit and they talked about a couple more things before hanging up. Knowing she had a few things to do to tidy up before he got there, Della raised herself from her seat and walked over to open the door. As she unlocked it, she felt a rush and nearly fell from the dizziness that followed. She grabbed onto a nearby table to break her fall and, after a few seconds, found her way to the couch, not noticing the immense swelling that had already begun in her hand.

Abraham finished his daily rounds at the hospital and began tying things up as he prepared to leave for the day. He went to the phone to call Della again to see if she needed anything before he got there, but there was no answer. He thought nothing more of it than the possibility of her having had to run some errands. Shortly after his phone call, Nancy called and since Della didn't answer, left a brief message. She found it kind of odd that she was not at the office or at home, but thought immediately that she must have been with Abraham. After hanging up the phone, and in a very snotty tone of voice she said aloud, "Figures. Why would I even think she'd be at home or have any time for 'friends'? That may take up too much of *Abraham's* time. And Heaven forbid we make things uncomfortable for him!" Although she would never admit it, Nancy was beside herself with pure jealousy. She couldn't stand the fact that Della had someone when she didn't. But Della never heard the phone ring. She was passed out on the couch. She had felt a little delirious before collapsing but didn't think much of it. Her hand continued to swell where the insect had bitten her and discoloration had begun. She lied limp and seemingly lifeless on the sofa. Time was passing but Della hadn't noticed. Neither had she noticed the low grade fever that had developed. Actually, she'd felt a little warm before passing out but paid no attention to that, either. She was so excited about the fact that Abraham was coming by that the feelings of elation seemed to cover up the impending sickness.

"One hundred point eight degrees," Driscelle said as she shook the thermometer. I'd better call Abraham. She picked up the phone and dialed the number. Abraham picked up on the first ring, thinking it was Della. Driscelle told him Little Abe was sick and that he needed to get over there right away. Immediately, he dialed Della's number.

"Sweetheart, I know we made plans for this evening but my son is sick. Driscelle just called and I need to get over there as soon as possible. I hope you get this message soon. I'll call you as soon as I know something."

Again, Della never heard the phone ring.

As Driscelle waited for Abraham to get there, her phone rang.

"Hey, Drissy.

"What's up, Mr. Married Man?" she answered sarcastically.

"Now how you gonna act like that," Fabian answered in his best Tyreese voice.

"Where's Wifey? Does she know you're calling me?"

"Come on, Drissy. Cut out the attitude."

"What do you want, Fabian?"

"Don't we have some unfinished business?"

"No, we don't have any business."

"I think we do."

"And what might that be? I don't recall calling you. If I remember correctly, my phone rang and when I picked it up, you were on the other end of my line. So the real question is, 'what do you want?'"

"You called me a few weeks ago wanting a favor..."

"And you weren't up for it so we have nothing to discuss. Go find your wife if you need conversation because I have none for you. Goodbye," she said sharply.

"Hold up, Little Girl," he said in a tone of voice she hadn't heard from him before.

"I think we need to talk about the paternity of one little boy named Abe."

"What?" Driscelle asked in utter shock. "What is that supposed to mean?"

"You know exactly what that means," he answered in a slurred tone that let her know he'd been drinking.

"I think you've been tipping that bottle a little bit too much. Why don't you hang up now and go find your wife because she's who you should be talking to about sons and paternity," she retorted.

"What you think is that you know it all. You've always thought you could outsmart us all, Drissy, but some of us are smarter than you think. The kid is mine and you've played this game with Homeboy long enough. I think it's time for me to collect what's mine, don't you think, Driscelle? Don't you think?"

"What I think is that you're crazy. That's what I think. I think..."

"No," he shouted, startling her. "You don't think, and that's your problem. You didn't think I was smart enough to count up the months from your pregnancy to the time the baby got here. You didn't think I would feel it when we made the baby. You didn't think I was smart enough to know what you were trying to do to that dude, Abraham, and you didn't think I was smart enough to know you were trying to use me. I'm not dumb, Drissy. I never was. I was just stupidly in love with you," he said as he began an alcohol induced cry. "But I ain't in love with you no more," he slurred.

"Are you crying? You've been drinking, you're crying and trying to run game on me. Your wife is not going to be happy about this. As a matter of fact, she's probably wondering where you are and you need to go tend to her needs and leave me alone with this nonsense..."

"There you go again," he shouted angrily, tears becoming more apparent. "You think you know everything. You don't know anything about me or my wife or anything. You think you're so smart. You've always thought you were better than the rest of us but you're not, Drissy. You are one of us and no uptown, high class apartment in a white neighborhood is going to change that!" By this time, he was really shouting.

"What do you want, Fabian? If you called to insult me, you shouldn't have wasted your dime. Maybe your wife puts up with this but I'm not that kind of girl. What? Did she go out for more beer and you needed someone to fill in for her? You need to go to the corner store and find her because this mess is for her, not me. Where is she anyway? At the beauty shop *gettin' her hair did* or something?" Driscelle laughed at herself as she did her best ghetto girl impression.

"If it's any of your business, which it isn't, she's in the hospital. We lost our son about four hours ago," he said as he completely broke down. "I don't know what to do, Drissy. I lost my boy. She started bleeding and we couldn't stop it. They couldn't stop it. I couldn't save him," he cried.

"Oh, my God. Stay there. I'll be right there. Where are you? Are you at the hospital or are you at home?"

"I'm at home. I'm here, at home, if that's what you want to call it. How can a man have a home with no children in it? Why did this happen to me? Drissy, bring me my boy."

"Stay there, I'm on my way," she said and hung up. It occurred to her that she didn't know where he lived and couldn't call him back. She knew his cell phone number, which was what she used to get in touch with him but she also knew the hood well enough to be able to ask someone to show her where he lived. That much she did know. She knew he still lived in their old hood. In the hood, you'd better know somebody or you'd better not be there. They knew her down there and they respected her. But if worse came to worse, she could always call his mother's house to find out the information she needed. His mother had always liked her and Driscelle knew it and, as with everything else, used it to her advantage.

She grabbed Little Abe, who really wasn't sick enough to have Abraham come over. She was just using that to get him there to satisfy her need to see him. Forgetting about the fact that he was on his way, or maybe just not caring, she grabbed her purse and the two of them headed over to find Fabian. She tore out of the driveway and down the street just missing Abraham who was to turn the corner five minutes after she did. When he got to her place and found it empty, he figured they must have gone to the hospital. He became frantic and headed to his place of employment. He knew he'd be able to find them with no problems. After getting there and asking a co-worker to look them up in the computer, he discovered they weren't there. He became even more worried and left the hospital to get back into his car. Not knowing where to go, it dawned on him that he had a cell phone and so did she. He got no answer when he dialed her number. He tried again and again and again. He drove back to her place hoping she'd gone back home but when he got there, her car was nowhere to be found and her apartment was dark.

He paced and paced outside her door for about an hour before deciding to go back home and wait.

In the meantime, Della lay on her couch, still passed out, completely unaware of all that was going on around her. Abraham called her to let her know about his situation and all he got was her answering machine. Again, he figured she'd stepped out, even though it struck him as odd. Because of his own emergency, he didn't have time to give it much thought. He kept calling Driscelle but never got an answer.

Driscelle had found Fabian, who was an absolute mess by the time she got there. As she figured, he had been drinking. He smelled of a saloon but worse than that, he was balled up in fetal position on the floor in the corner of his apartment. In all her years of knowing him, she'd never seen him in such a state. By the time they'd gotten there, Little Abe had fallen asleep so she had to carry him in. She put him down on the couch in the living room and went to tend to Fabian. Things hadn't changed much in his routine. The spare key to his apartment was where he'd always left it. In her own vanity, the thought crossed her mind that he'd left it there hoping she'd surprise him someday and use it. Letting herself into his apartment was no problem. The furniture was the same, almost as she'd left it, and that, for whatever reason, was kind of eerie to her. Nevertheless, she found him and the site wasn't pretty. He'd drank himself into oblivion and had passed out. She covered him up and started making phone calls to old friends to see if anybody knew anything. What she found out was that Atina had been to work and upon returning home, felt liquid running down her legs. After having run to the bathroom to help herself, she made the call to 911. She also called Fabian who'd arrived shortly before the ambulance came. The cause of the miscarriage was not known. Driscelle debated whether or not to go to the hospital to see her before deciding to stay away. She didn't want to take Little Abe in there nor did she want any drama to get started. She knew she couldn't pick Fabian up so she left him on the floor, locked up the apartment and called his sister to let her know she'd been there and about the condition her brother was in. She and her son had just begun the ride back home when she looked over at him and saw what everybody else already knew. The resemblance between the boy and his father was very strong. It was as if his father had chewed him up and spit him out. There was really no need for a paternity test. Genes and chromosomes had already proven that point. It was a good thing that Abraham and Fabian didn't know each other. It was even better that there were no mutual friends. No one to spill the beans; at least for now. Driscelle found herself in a tight spot. Had the tables been turned on her? Abraham thought he was the father and now she discovers Fabian's thinking of the same thing. Would either of them find out the truth? All they had to do was see one another. The answer would be obvious. Suddenly, Driscelle felt an urge to relocate.

THIRTY

By morning, Abraham had finally made contact with Driscelle, who blew the whole situation off. She told him she'd had an emergency that had nothing to do with her son and that he shouldn't have been so frantic. She was referring to the number of missed calls on her cell phone, which she'd left in the car while in Fabian's apartment, as well as the number of messages he'd left on her answering machine and voicemail.

"You could have had the decency to call me," he said angrily.

"Well, I had so much going on my end that I didn't think about you. I'm sorry."

"That's your problem, Driscelle. You don't think," he stammered.

Driscelle almost laughed at the insult that seemed reminiscent of her phone call from the day before. She got him off the phone and began fixing a meal for her son and herself to eat before they started their day.

Abraham, incensed by Driscelle's irresponsibility and inconsideration, decided to stop by Della's on his way to work. He called and still got no answer. As he approached her house, he saw her car in the driveway. As he approached the door, he was startled to find it slightly ajar. He pushed his way in and began screaming for her. It didn't take long to find her as she was still passed out on the couch. He ran over to her and began shaking her and checking for a pulse. She uttered a few strange sounds as she began to awaken. Relieved to find her alive, he rolled her over onto her back. Instantly, he spotted her hand which looked like it had been pumped up with helium! It almost looked like it could float in the air if given the chance. He became alarmed and began the process of waking her. She gave off signs that she was going to be okay. After coming to, it was obvious that she was a little delirious and somewhat disoriented. It seemed as if her coloring was a little off, which was hard to describe. She looked as if she'd had an orange-- or maybe a reddish-orange- -tint to her. Without asking any questions, Abraham cleaned her up as best he could and transported her to the hospital emergency room where, after a few hours, he learned of the insect bite and its effects on her. Fortunately for her, the venom of the insect wasn't deadly. It seemed to have a sleep induction quality in humans that, in other species, caused a paralysis necessary for escape from predators. The hospital had seen many of these before and the season was right for it. No anecdote was necessary and there was no danger of permanent damage. Della would need to rest for at least twenty-four hours and drink plenty of fluids. The doctor suggested light foods as vomiting was common in bite victims of the insect and advised a cold pack for the swelling. Della was released to go home even though the disorientation hadn't completely cleared up. Abraham wasn't sure whether or not Della even knew what was going on. She was quiet and in and out of consciousness. Abraham was quite concerned and slightly down. He felt that if he'd gone to see her as he promised, things wouldn't have been as bad for her as they'd been. The truth be known, there was nothing he could have done. The effect of the insect's venom had to run its course and once bitten, there was nothing anyone could do except wait, and that's just what Abraham did. He waited with her until he had to go back to work. He tucked her in bed, made some soup and kept it for her until she woke up. No sooner than that happened, the phone rang.

"Hello".

"Oh, I'm sorry. I must have the wrong number."

"Who are you looking for," Abraham asked.

"Is this 555-7979?" Nancy asked.

"Yes, it is."

"Is the lady of the house home?"

"Yes, she is, but she's not available right now. May I ask who's calling?"

"This is a close friend of hers and the real question is who's answering her phone? I know you don't live there because I don't recognize your voice."

"This is Abraham. With whom am I speaking?"

"Oh," she said dryly as if she wanted him to know that she had a problem with him. "This is Nancy. Tell her that I returned her call," she said and hung up before he could respond.

"Boy, she certainly is no 'Miss Congeniality'," he said and hung up the phone.

Della was in and out of sleep and would periodically try to talk but could only utter sounds. As Abraham started toward her room, the phone rang again. Thinking it might be Nancy calling back, he braced himself. "Hello," he answered.

"Hi, is Della home?"

"Yes, she is, but she can't come to the phone right now."

"Who's this?"

"This is Abraham. Who is this?"

"Oh, hi, Abraham. This is Patricia. Della has told me so much about you. How are you today?"

"I'm fine, thanks. Hey, tell her that I called, would you? I don't want to waste too much of your time."

"Patricia, wait. Della is not feeling well and I think she needs someone to be here with her. I have to go back to work in a little while but I really don't want to leave her here all by herself. Do you know of anyone I could call for her?"

"What's wrong with her?"

"She was bitten by some kind of insect and her hand is three times its normal size. I took her to the emergency room earlier to make sure she was okay and the bite was confirmed. Its venom has made her drowsy and there will probably be some nausea, vomiting and possibly fever by the time she wakes up."

"I'll be right there," she said and they exchanged good-byes.

Pleased that someone she could trust was going to be there with his dear Della, Abraham hung up the phone and went in to sit with her. As he watched her sleep, he reflected back on the two phone calls, which basically equated to the differences in the two friends. "Boy, Nancy seems like a dragon lady, but Patricia seems so sweet. I wonder why that is," he thought as he tried to shrug it off and go on about his business. But there was something about the call from Nancy that just wouldn't let him go.

THIRTY-ONE

Nancy lied in bed staring at the ceiling, trying to make heads or tails of what had transpired in her life over the last several months. Self-reflection was something she did often, but this time was different. Usually she could point fingers and place blame on everyone else, and be right about it, but this time she had to take a look at herself. She'd lost two of her best friends, one who left a young daughter who had already lost a parent. Sure Angie had been too young to know Cliff, but that didn't change the fact that she had been left without at least one natural parent. Cliff had succumbed to throat cancer only a few years before China had expired.

She'd also been separated from her other two friends for reasons that weren't quite as clear. Patricia had become the resident pastor, which Nancy had had enough of growing up, and Della had fallen in love like some sick little puppy. There was no one left of the group. Only months ago, everything seemed wonderful. They were in a club doing the girl thing when all of a sudden the news of Abrie's accident changed their lives forever. Things could never, ever be the same. Even if Abrie fully recovered, China would never return and it would never be the same again. So where did that leave the group? What was friendship all about and did we, as human beings, put too much emphasis on friendship?

And then there was Ross. Ross was a good man and Nancy realized that her feelings for him were out of control. They were deeper than she'd realized, but were they genuine? Maybe they were there because she was so lonely. She wondered if she really cared about Ross as she drifted off to sleep, dreaming that she was calling his name.

"Ross. Ross," Amos shouted as he banged on his brother's car window. Ross had driven home from his office and fallen asleep in the car after having parked in his parking space. He felt delirious and didn't even realize how long he had been there. Amos had come by the apartment building to fix some things for one of the other tenants when he noticed his brother sleeping in his car.

"Man, are you okay?"

"Yeah. What time is it?"

"It's almost eight o'clock. What are you doing out here?" Amos asked expressing genuine concern.

"I don't know. I guess I must have been tired. I remember parking the car and taking a minute to think and the next thing I knew, you were banging on my window like a raving lunatic. Man what's wrong with you?" Ross laughed.

"Well, it's not every day you see your brother sleeping outside of his apartment in his car," he laughed. "I guess not much has changed at the Ponderosa, huh?"

"Oh, man, if you need the unit, I can have my stuff out of here by..."

"Be serious. Partner, you pay rent. I don't need you to move," he quipped. "You're one of the best tenants I have because if you skip out, I know how to find you. Stay as long as you want."

Both of the men laughed, which was good because they both needed it. Amos was worried about Ross. He knew things weren't good between him and Marlena, and he honestly didn't feel that they'd ever get back together. He wasn't sure that he'd hoped they did, either. He had nothing against Marlena, but he'd never approved of the marriage from the beginning and he knew his brother needed more than what he was getting from it. He knew his brother was a very sensitive, caring man and had been through too much already. Marlena was not the kind of woman who could give him what he deserved. Before he realized it, he heard himself asking Ross, "Have you called her?"

"No, and it's been a while."

"Man what are you waiting for? You've got to do something. You need to make some decisions. You don't look good, and after today's incident, I'm getting a little concerned. I don't mean to get in your business but you're going downhill."

"You're right. You really are and I can't argue with you. I just don't know what to do or what to say."

"What do you want to do?"

"I really don't know, but I don't think I want to go back. In fact, I know I don't want to go back. This relationship has not been healthy for me; it never has been and I don't know that things will ever get any better. Too much damage has been done."

"Man that sounds kind of serious. Do you realize what you're saying?"

"Amos, I've known for a long time that this relationship wasn't right, but I just didn't want to admit it. I hadn't intended to admit it a minute ago, either, but it just came out."

At that moment, Ross' cell phone began to ring. He'd forgotten to turn it off as he usually did every day after work. He looked at it, recognized his home phone number and hesitated to answer when he heard Amos ask, "Is it her?"

Nodding his head "yes", Amos encouraged him to go ahead and take the phone call, so he did.

"Ross?"

"Yes, Marlena."

"Ross, where have you been? I've been trying to get in touch with you for weeks but you haven't been responding to my calls. I've left message after message..."

"What do you want, Marlena? Why did you call?" He interrupted her as if he were talking to a bothersome customer. Amos heard his brother's tone and felt it his cue to leave, so he did just that. He waved and walked to his car. Ross waved back and began walking toward his apartment.

"Ross, why are you so cold? What's with you? You know we need to talk. I haven't seen you at the rehab center and they are about to send Abrie home..."

"I've been there. I just haven't been attending those family sessions because I've had enough."

"What about us?" Marlena asked abruptly.

"What *about* us?" Ross replied.

"We do have a marriage to tend to, you know. I know that things are strained and I haven't been the best wife I could have been, but we can work things out. We need to talk. What about a second chance?"

"A second chance at what, Marlena? I tried for years to make things work. I suffered, sacrificed and settled. I didn't even know who I was any more. At least I didn't until now. I'm starting to feel like the man who had to die in order to survive his relation-ship. I don't know if I can do that to myself again. Marlena, I want to live and I want to live as a man. Not some pansy for a hardcore medical examiner who treats everyone in her life as if they were dead. I am not a corpse. My heart is still beating and I'm not brain dead. I don't want to live like that!"

"Baby, must we talk about this over the phone? Can we meet somewhere to discuss this face to face? It doesn't have to be at the house. We can meet at a restaurant or somewhere mutual."

For a second or two, both of them were stunned to hear the desperation in her voice. She hadn't called him "Baby" in years. She had shown no affection at all for him in years.

"No. No, Marlena. I'm not ready yet."

"Then when, Ross? When? When are you ever going to be ready?"

"I don't know, Marlena. I don't know if I'll ever be ready."

Shocked and surprised, Marlena let out an audible sigh.

"I have to go," Ross said. "The only issue I *want* to talk to you about we haven't discussed yet, and that is Abrie. I know that extensive work still needs to be done to help her to recover. I talked to her case manager last week. I would be willing to take care of her if..."

"Ross, what are you saying? You can't be for real and I am not going to discuss my daughter with you over the phone!"

"*Your* daughter? I think you mean *our* daughter. I may not have gotten much from this marriage but I did get three wonderful children and I'm not about to turn my back on them now. I think we need to discontinue this conversation now and pick it up later..."

"When? When, Ross?" she shouted. "You won't talk to me and if you think you are going to get my daughter than you'd better think again!"

"Now I know it's time for me to go. I'm going to hang up right now and we will continue this discussion later," he said and before she could utter another sound, he had hung up the phone.

Unhappy with the way things turned out, she let out a scream that even sounded funny to her. She felt as if her whole world was caving in and there was nothing she could do about it. She felt out of control and that was an odd feeling for her. Ross seemed relentless and unmerciful and Marlena could not figure out what she'd done to deserve his treatment of her. In frustration, she cried. She threw the cordless phone she'd been using, balled up into a corner on their king sized bed and cried like a baby. Things were not working out as she'd planned. She figured Ross would have been back by now and things would have been manageable for her--for them. Marlena felt helpless.

Meanwhile, things were getting better for Abrie. Therapy was going well and her discharge date was vastly approaching. She was making two to three word sentences and was showing better manual dexterity. Her rehab team was astonished at her progress and felt pretty good about themselves. What they didn't feel so sure of was the environment she was about to be released to. They knew what lied ahead for the family and things didn't appear to be going as well on the home front as they were in the clinic.

THIRTY-TWO

PATRICIA AND ABRAHAM HAD FINALLY met face to face but under circumstances neither of them appreciated. Patricia had relieved Abraham of his watch and assumed the position. Della seemed to be doing okay. Abraham had been told to watch for fever and any other significant changes but, fortunately, there was no change for the worse. Patricia had a good feeling that the worse was over and that Della would be okay. She sat next to her friend's bed and thanked God that He hadn't taken another of her friends. As she went to do a "just-in-case" fever check, the phone rang.

"Hey, Patricia. It's Abraham. How's my girl doing?"

"Oh, she's just fine. I think the worse is over because she seems to be sleeping very peacefully. She doesn't seem to be doing the "in and out" thing and her breathing seems normal. There's no sign of fever, either."

"You sound like you're in the wrong business."

"I beg your pardon?"

"If I didn't know better, I'd think you belonged here with the rest of us med-heads."

They both laughed.

"Hey, Patricia, may I confide in you?"

"Sure, if it's not too deep."

"Well, it's kind of deep but I think you can handle it. You seem to have a level head and I really need to talk to someone about this."

"Fire away."

"I panicked today. I thought I had lost her. That was an awful feeling for me. You know, you never know how deeply you feel for a person until something like this happens. I thought I was moving too fast because I am normally very, very cautious in a situation like this. Lord knows I've had my bumps and bruises in the love department. Patricia, I've felt from the time I laid eyes on her that I loved her and I know you probably don't believe in love at first sight, but I know that's what it was and after today, I can't help but know that this is the woman I want to spend the rest of my life with. When I found her on that sofa, I felt like one side of me was paralyzed. I felt like half of me was gone. Nothing in life has ever made me feel that way but I don't want her to think I'm making a rash decision about what I'm going to say."

After a long pause, Patricia asked, "What is it exactly that you want to say?"

"Patricia, I want to marry Della. It doesn't have to be today or tomorrow. It can be whenever she wants to do it but I want to marry her. I never thought I would ever feel this way about anyone. This is it for me. My mother always told me that when I met that one, I'd know. She said I'd know because my spirit would leap inside me every time I'd see, hear or touch that one. This is it for me."

"Well, Abraham, I've known Della for a long time and I can't tell you what a good choice you've made. She is a good person and I'll tell you what. If I were a man, I'd want to marry her myself!"

They both laughed and chit-chatted for a few more minutes before getting off the phone. The conversation between the two of them flowed very smoothly, leaving them feeling like they'd known each other for a long time. No more than three minutes after hanging up, the phone rang again. Almost skipping to speak again to the one she'd deemed the world's sweetest and most sincere guy, Patricia gleefully answered the phone.

"Hel-lo."

"Hey, who's this?"

"Hey, Nancy. It's me. Patricia."

"Hey, girl. What are you doing over there?"

"I'm on fever-watch."

"Fever-watch? What does that mean?"

"Della was bitten by some insect and she passed out. Her hand swelled like a hot-air balloon and Abraham, who found her, took her to the hospital. She's been groggy and in and out of sleep, but seems to be resting peacefully now. Abraham was told to stay with her and watch for fever but he had to go to work, so I'm here."

"Oh, he couldn't stay with her, huh? You mean 'lover boy' couldn't handle his business?"

"No, 'lover boy' had to go to work and he handled his business before he left. What's eating you?"

"Nothing. I was just wondering why he couldn't stay with her when she needed him. He's with her any other time."

"Ooo, you sound jealous. Sounds like someone has been sippin' on some HATERADE! Nancy, I know *you're* not jealous. You have to be happy for the girl. She's been through a lot and if any one deserves to be happy, it's Della. You're just mad cuz you ain't got nobody," Patricia said and shrieked with laughter. "Your day is coming, Honey. You just have to quit being so hateful and get on your knees and ask The Big Guy for what you want. You know what to do cuz I'm sure your daddy has explained it to you."

"Whatever," Nancy said hatefully. "I'm not jealous of some little immature guy who can't even eat breakfast without Della. I mean, he's with her all the time. Why can't he be with her now?"

"You're one of her best friends. Why aren't you with her? You've known her longer than he has but you're not here due to other obligations, right? The man had to go to work and besides, she'd need him if none of her friends were available. I just happened to be in a position where I could relieve him and he could go to work. It's not like he left her to go hang out with his partners. You need to quit sippin'."

"Whatever. How's she doing?"

"She's fine, but not as fine as she's going to be when she wakes up."

"What's that supposed to mean?"

"'Lover boy' just called and told me he wants to marry her, and I am so excited for them."

"What?" Nancy asked dryly.

"You heard, Haterella. He wants to marry her and I know she's going to say 'yes'."

"You don't know that. They hardly know each other and he is so immature. He needs to grow up," she snapped.

"No, you need to *put up*. You need to put up that cup of haterade because you're going to choke on it soon! What's with you?"

"Whatever. You sound as childish as he does."

"Is it that I'm childish or that you're jealous? Your problem, Nancy, is that you're too serious about life. You need to take a chill pill. You always think everything good is supposed to come to you first. Well, Della beat you to the punch because she's loving and loveable. You're hateful, you're prudish and as a matter of fact, you're pretty stuck-up and you need to get over it and start being a friend and be happy for her instead of acting out your jealousy."

"You know something, Patricia?"

"Yep," she interrupted. "I know the truth hurts but the good news is that it shall also make you free. Face it, Nancy. You're just jealous and if you'd take your eyes off Ross Paterson, you'd find you a good man just like Della did."

"What did you say?" Nancy asked in total shock.

"I said, 'if you'd take your eyes off Ross Paterson, you'd find yourself one like Della did'. I didn't stutter. You heard me right the first time. You see, Nancy, if I've learned nothing else from everything we've been through over the last several months, it's that life is full of surprises and can be shorter than you think. With that, you don't always get second chances so you'd better be real with it the first time around. I've known for a long time that you've had the hots for Ross. You guys always thought that because I was the quietest in the group, I was also the dumbest. I'm not dumb. I've always noticed the way you'd glow whenever the man came around. I don't know whether or not the others noticed because I've never discussed it with them, but I'd always see the change in your behavior at even the sound of his name. I chose never to say anything about it but that makes me as guilty as you, so now I'm going to do my part. Nancy, a relationship with Ross Paterson will mean nothing but trouble for you. Stay away from the man. Especially now because he is very, very vulnerable. Della told me that he came to your house the other morning. What do you think he was there for? Quiet does not mean stupid; it means observant. Leave the man alone. You're headed for a danger zone that is not worth your while."

Stunned and absolutely dumbfounded, all Nancy could say was, "You know what Patricia? You're absolutely right."

After an awkward silence, Patricia qualified her speech by explaining that she'd been quiet for too long and sat by as an accomplice as the girls had done many things they shouldn't have. She told of how she'd compromised her morals and values just to have friends and that it wasn't worth it to her any more. If being honest would cost her the friendships of the one's she loved the most, than that was just the way it would have to be because honesty was quite liberating for her. Nancy listened quietly and took heed to everything her friend had said. Under normal circumstances, she would have blown up and gotten crazy, but she knew that her friend was right. Upon hanging up, she had a newfound respect for Patricia, not only as a friend but as a woman of God. She knew where this had come from because Patricia had found her place in the Lord. Nancy knew and could relate because she had compromised her morals and values, too. She knew what it was like to be a preacher's kid and have to hide the goodness you'd been taught for the sake of friendship and, for the first time in her life, she felt she had a real friend.

THIRTY-THREE

AFTER A TRYING AND TIRING shift, Abraham decided to call it a day. Before the days of Della, it was customary for him to stay around the hospital, almost working two shifts, on any given day. Over the last few months, days like that were few and far between for him. Today was definitely not going to be one of those days. He clocked out and left the hospital on time but not empty handed. With him was an envelope with lab results in it. He was reluctant to open it because he didn't want to be alone when he found out the news. He'd made up in his mind on the day the blood was drawn that Della would be the one to break the news to him. He wanted her to open the envelope and read the results to him, knowing he was going to take it hard either way, and that she'd know exactly how to comfort him. But things had changed. He didn't anticipate Della having had the problem she'd had nor did he ever think she wouldn't be available to him when he needed her. This caused him to sit in his car for a few minutes and do some real soul searching. The thought of losing Della put some

things on his mind. What if he lost Little Abe, too?
Regardless of the results of the test, Little Abe would
always be his son, but that was before the information
became cast in stone. He knew that the contents of that
envelope would change his life forever and he wasn't
ready for that. He put the results on the dashboard
of his car and began the route to Della's house. Upon
arrival, he had made some major decisions. Actually,
the choices had been pondered upon for months and
the finalization of them took place during the time it
took him to drive from the hospital to his destination.
He made it to her house, got out of the car and relieved
Patricia from duty, thanking her profusely for being the
friend she was. Della was still sleeping, "although," as
Patricia reported, she'd been "up for a few minutes to an
hour and even ate a little soup." As she slept, Abraham
began to talk to her about what he'd decided.

"Babe," he began. "I did a lot of thinking today and
I've decided that I'm not going to open the envelope
with the test results in it. I really don't want to know.
I am the only father Little Abe knows and I know that
if I find out he's not mine, things are going to change,
and I don't want that. He's been my son for almost five
years now and he and I have a good relationship. I want
that to always be. However, I am not going to throw
the results away. I am going to keep them in a safe place
should the need to open the envelope ever arise. I am
going to continue to pay child support, but I am going
to have more control over how the money is spent. If
Driscelle wants to contest this, we'll have to open up
the results. Somehow I get the feeling that she'll want
them to remain sealed. I don't know why I feel that, I

just do. I don't know how you are going to feel about this, but I am confident you will support and respect my decision. That's one of the reasons I love you so much and want to spend the rest of my life with you. I think it's best that things be left as they are. I want to leave well enough alone. Besides, you two get along so well that I'm sure he won't mind you being the new edition to the family."

At that, Della moaned a little and shifted her body and her head as if to let him know she was still alive but not quite awake. He took a look at her hand and couldn't tell if any progress had been made. He hopped on the bed, shaking it unintentionally and lied down next to her. He hadn't been that comfortable in bed in years. Before he knew it, he had fallen asleep. Being near Della always made him feel like he was floating on a cloud.

Patricia sang all the way home. She was so excited about what Abraham had shared with her, but was more excited about having put Nancy in her place. She'd waited years to check Nancy on the situation with Ross. The reason she hadn't before was because he had never made any passes at her friend and he had never, to her knowledge, responded to any of her advances. In her heart of hearts she knew Nancy was wrong, but had for years rationalized her own bystander apathy with the lack of proof that anything had or would ever happen.

Today, however, was different. Patricia felt she had won one for the Kingdom. If that truth were half as liberating for Nancy as it was for her, Nancy would feel a few pounds lighter. In thinking about it, Patricia figured it had to be weighing Nancy down. After having heard the bitterness and jealousy in her friend's voice, she knew that something had to change.

As for Ross, Patricia couldn't figure out why on God's green earth, the man had gone to Nancy's place, but was grateful to God that nothing had happened. She knew her friend and knew how vulnerable she was when it came to him. In all her years of knowing Nancy, she'd never seen anything weaken her like Ross Paterson could. The man could come near Nancy and have her melt like ice, but even though they'd referred to Marlena as "The Ice Princess" from time to time, Patricia knew that an affair between her husband and her daughter's friend would be just enough to turn that ice into fire, and the fallout from that wouldn't ever be worth it.

Nancy went into the bathroom and washed her face. She felt disgusting and decided to take a shower. After entering into the tepid water, she began scrubbing and scrubbing and scrubbing her skin as if she could wash off the filth of the idea of an adulterous affair. She began to cry. She couldn't believe that, after all this time, she had been preserving her heart for a married man. Not just any married man; the father of a close friend of hers. For the first time since it began, she stopped to think about how it would have effected Abrie. The thought also crossed her mind about the devastation it would have left on the whole group of friends. Even if she and Ross had gallivanted off into the sunset together, never to be seen again, it still would have left a strain on the group; guilt by association in the eyes of Marlena Paterson. She wouldn't have wanted any more of Abrie's friends around. The guilt that poor Abrie would have felt for bringing this man snatcher around would have been enough to do her in. Finally, the anger Marlena would have had against Abrie would have messed the family up for generations. She couldn't believe she would have risked all of her friends for a man who was off limits to her. She cried as she realized these and one other very relevant thing: her daddy. For many more years than her own affair of the heart, she had accused her own father of something she now knew he would have never done. She needed to apologize to him for it, but how? When? She knew she had to do it during the time she was spending with her parents because as Patricia said, "sometimes you don't get second chances". For all she knew, this could be the last chance for her to patch things up with him. She was not going to gamble. She needed to take another step in rekindling the flame with her father. She was aware of how difficult it would be for her: as difficult as swallowing pride.

THIRTY-FOUR

DRISCELLE SAT STARING OUT THE window at the beautiful landscaping around her apartment. There was a park across the street and several families were enjoying quality time together. Lost inside her thoughts, she didn't hear the laughter of the kids, the cracking sound of the bat hitting the baseball, the swish of the basketball scoring or the yelling and screaming of the happy little girls who were playing foot games on the grass. She couldn't even hear her own thoughts.

A few days had passed and she found herself wondering about Atina. Even though the girl had taken her "stash", they *had* been friends for quite some time before then. Atina *had* been her best friend at one time and regardless of the things that had recently transpired between them, no woman deserved to go through this. She wondered if Atina was alone or if family was with her. She knew the woman would get no support; at least, not the kind one would need in a situation like this because things are different in the hood. You go through something and people are by your side, but then, it's over. It's not like what goes on uptown. Uptown folk are by your side and they support you in a different kind of way. They want to make sure you get back together mentally and emotionally, as well as physically, but in the hood, you just bounce back. Once it's over, it's over. Sometimes they don't understand that the pain that goes way down deep needs to come out of there. It's not healthy to just bury it and act as though it doesn't matter anymore. When you do that, other things get piled on top of it and before you know it, all of your issues start running together without you realizing that the first issue is directly connected to all of the other stuff. And people wonder why therapists lie you down on a couch and ask you about your childhood. It's to get down to the *real* issue because all of the rest of them are just symptoms of that one. If you've ever been traumatized, all of the other stuff that happens after that can be directly linked to the first ordeal, if you don't get help for it.

Driscelle found herself reminiscing about her childhood and all of the safety issues she had then. She remembered being scared as a child because she had to be the adult in the house, which is often what happens to the oldest child of an alcoholic/addict. She found herself linking all of the things she did with Fabian, Abraham and a host of other men to the insecurity placed in her as a child. Her wickedness was the result of her fear of loving, which was the direct result of her not wanting anyone to hurt her the way her mother did. She loved her mother, but her mother hurt her desperately. Her mother hurt her more than once and every time she forgave her, she left herself open to be hurt again; all direct hits because she never protected herself. As soon as she began protecting herself, the hits weren't as painful. She found that by protecting herself, she could take a hit; and another and another and another and after awhile, it didn't hurt anymore. The saddest part of it all was that her protection was found in the hardening of her heart and not allowing herself to love anyone. Her life's ambition became protecting herself from hurt. Without hurt, she felt secure. Protection from hurt meant control. You learn to control yourself, the one you "love", and all of the moves that are made in the relationship.

With tears streaming down her face, she felt herself say, "All I wanted was to *be loved* and to know that I *was loved*. That's all I ever wanted and that's what would have made me feel safe."

As she realized what she was feeling, she shook herself and said, "Come on, Girl. You've got to get yourself together. You're not that soft and you know better." At that, she got up from her seat and went in to check on Little Abe, who had been in the living room watching television for the last couple of hours.

Atina had been released from the hospital after having been there only a couple of days. Fabian, who felt she should have been in for much longer, refused to leave her side. For most of the day, he sat at her bedside with his head on her lap and his arms hugging her legs. It was as if he felt that by doing that, he could keep her alive. To Atina, it was sweet but somewhat sickening. She really didn't want to be touched but wanted even less to reject the man she loved more than life itself. She grieved the loss of the baby but wasn't sure which was more painful; that or the fact that what she saw as her security with Fabian was now gone. What she didn't know was that she had all the security she needed because Fabian truly did love her. At times he was confused, but it was the unconditional love she gave to him that caused it. He'd never had it before and wasn't used to it. That made him skeptical at times and as a result of that, he'd stay emotionally close to the door in case he needed to run. He understood Driscelle. He didn't love her but he knew her. She was predictable and he knew when she was on the verge of doing something that would devastate him. As painful as it was, he stuck with it because he could see it coming and consequently, brace himself. It was like living in hurricane country. As devastating as the hurricanes are, you know when they are coming and you prepare yourself for them. When the storm hits, you don't know how bad it's going to be, but you have somewhat of an idea. Once it's over, you observe the aftermath, get over the shock and immediately begin to put things back together again, but you don't leave the region where you live. You just learn to live there--and Fabian had learned to live with Driscelle. Atina didn't understand it and he couldn't explain it, but fortunately for him, she'd made the commitment to stay and weather the storms.

Neither of them realized that the events in their lives that caused them so much pain, such as the loss of the baby, were the very things that were drawing them closer together and pushing Driscelle completely out. We always question why God allows such tragedy but when you look at the human condition, it's the only time we really pay attention. Tragedy is what causes us to take Him seriously. When things are going good, we say "tomorrow. Okay, God, I know You're there, but I'll do what You want me to do tomorrow." Or we say, "God, You know what I need so why won't You help me?" When He answers in subtle ways, we attribute it to our own doing, our circumstances or the "natural progression of things". Many even credit nature--as if you can really separate the two. But let God allow something to happen that causes pain or inconvenience. The first thing we say is, "Oh, my God" or "Oh, Lord, how could You do this?" Lamentations 3:32-33 tells us that though He brings grief, He doesn't enjoy it. Sometimes He has to bring pain to get us to pray to Him in order to give us what He knows we're going to need, and Atina *had* been praying for closeness in her marriage. She wanted Fabian to appreciate her and love her more than Driscelle. God had been trying to show her that He was indeed listening, but every time He'd send something to show her that it was on the way, she'd take her eyes off Him and turn to Driscelle. In doing that, she'd become frantic and come up with her own plan to defeat her in order to win the affection of her husband. When we put our own plan into effect, how can we expect *God's* plan to ever work? If we had to do it on our own, why would there be a need to pray about anything, or for that matter, why would we need God? In scripture we are told to "be still and know that He is God". We are also told that the weapons of our warfare are not carnal and that no weapon formed against us shall prosper because we are more than conquerors, and if God be for us, who can be against us? If we'd only believe what He says to us.

Driscelle decided to stay in the room with Little Abe and before she knew it, she was staring at him. It was as if she was seeing him for the first time--and she *really* was. For the first time in his life, she saw him as a child; not an insurance plan. *An insurance plan!*

The thought rushed her like a defensive lineman with an opening to sack the quarterback. It dawned on her that she hadn't been much better a mother to him than her mother had been to her. The only difference was that her mother had a tangible excuse. Almost in one motion, she stood up, lunged toward Little Abe and threw her arms around him. The little boy did not respond in the way she thought he would; he only moved his head around hers so that he could see the television. There was no return of affection because she had not taught him to respond to her in that way. Whenever he tried to be affectionate with her, she pushed him away and either verbally or non-verbally, and sometimes both, told him to go away. It had been that way all of his life.

Suddenly her mind went back to the day she went to pick Little Abe up from Abraham's house. She remembered them rolling around on the floor and the excitement in his eyes when his dad walked into the room. Not only did he return the affection; he expected it. He waited for it because he knew that Abraham would give it to him. Her son had learned to love and expect love from Abraham, but not from her.

A barrage of childhood memories of rejection flooded her mind. The pain came upon her like a tidal wave. She remembered being curled up in a corner in her closet wishing and wanting to be held. There were vivid memories of her being really afraid and needing to feel her mother close, but that kind of closeness was not available to her. "What have I done to you?" she whispered.

Little Abe did not respond, in part because he didn't hear her but also because, unless she was screaming and cussing, he didn't expect her to be talking to him. Talking with him was not something she did often. In fact, when the two of them were home together, there was rarely any conversation. The lack of response on his part caused her to reach for the child within her. That "child" is what helped her to understand how her son must have been feeling and for that, she began to sob. Little Abe looked up at her with contemplation on his face. He wasn't sure whether or not it was okay to help her. The contemplation quickly turned to fear and at that moment, she realized her son was afraid of *her*! And rightfully so since she did nothing but scold, demand, push, punish and criticize him on a regular basis. Who wouldn't have been afraid of a mother like that at four years old? For that matter, who, at any age wouldn't have been afraid or at the very least, annoyed? Driscelle knew then that things had to change, and for the first time in her life, she was serious about doing something to correct her mistakes.

THIRTY-FIVE

"HERE WE GO," MARLENA MUMBLED to herself as she stepped into the suit she'd chosen to wear for the day. A family therapy session was scheduled for 9:00 that morning and she was preparing herself mentally and physically for it. On the agenda was the date of Abrie's release with a treatment program designed to help transition her from 100% in-house rehabilitation. This plan would involve "trained professionals visiting the patient in the home to integrate her into non-institutionalized living and to teach the primary caretakers how to properly meet the patient's needs". The "primary caretakers" meant Ross and Marlena unless they hired a home health nurse for her. The problem was that Marlena didn't know what to do. She didn't know whether or not Ross was going to be home and she knew he'd have something to say if she went ahead and made plans to take care of it without him.

"What am I doing?" she asked herself. "Why should I care about what Ross thinks? If he isn't cooperating and he's 'not ready' to talk about it, why should I even consider him in this decision?" As if on key, a voice inside her said, "because he's your husband and he has a right to help with the decision making." "But he isn't acting like a husband," she said to the voice. "Have you been acting like a wife?"

Startled by the answers from within, Marlena shook her head as if to shake the voice away, but was left somewhat perplexed for the rest of the day. She'd never had conversation like that with herself and wondered who the mysterious voice of reason was. The saddest part of it all was that she knew it couldn't have been her because, not only did she never listen to anyone, but never gave anyone a chance to talk; especially if the speaker wanted to advise her on something. That was not the way she operated. Democracy was not the name of the game for her for she was and would always be a dictator. Nobody told her what to do *or* gave her unsolicited advice. Nobody. Not even Ross and now she found herself listening and to an *inner voice*, of all things.

She hurried to finish getting dressed as if in doing so, she would dodge the voice and not have to deal with the thought of being considerate of others. After all, had she not been considerate of Reggie, he'd be alive today.

On the drive to the center, she wondered if Ross would actually show up, and found herself secretly hoping against hope that he would. She missed him terribly and really needed him for support. It seemed that the more she dealt with her feelings about Reggie, the more she longed for Ross. She needed someone there, even if he couldn't be seen.

No sooner than she completed that thought, she couldn't believe what her eyes saw. Ross was crossing the lot to the rehabilitation center! He was there and for that, she was eternally grateful. She felt the void in her heart being filled as she had the desire to park her car in the middle of the street and run out to get to him. Resisting that desire was a lot harder than she would have ever imagined, and Marlena realized that her heart of ice was finally melting. The emotions that accompanied that revelation were mixed; glee, gladness, fear and sadness all wrapped in one. She paused for a moment to analyze her feelings for the purpose of figuring out what to do. Out of nowhere, the words of her therapist rang loudly in her mind, "stop analyzing everything and begin to feel. You are not an android. You *are* a human being but you won't let anyone get close enough to you to see that. Stop thinking and start feeling. Go with what you feel, Marlena. You, too, have a right to feel. Treat yourself at least once during your stay here on earth; be a human being. You might decide you like it!"

"Mr. Paterson, how nice to see you this morning," the therapist cooed.

Ross nodded and returned the greeting. As he was doing so, Abrie was being rolled in and her reaction to seeing him would have warmed the soul of any man. Her eyes lit up like Christmas tree lights as she shrieked with joy and nearly leaped out of her wheelchair. She began clapping her hands and audibly demonstrating her excitement about him being there. Ross hugged her and expressed his delight at seeing her. As he returned to a standing posture, a tear rolled down his cheek and Marlena appeared in the doorway. Another tear rolled down his cheek. Within minutes, the tears were streaming down his face. The therapist guided him to a chair and ushered him into it while motioning for Marlena to come over and sit next to him. As if on cue, the aide wheeled Abrie over to them and stopped her chair between Marlena and the therapist. The changed look on Abrie's face, coupled with the way she had been looking at Ross, suggested very strongly that she knew something was going on. Intense sadness marked her expression, prompt- ing the therapist to begin the session.

"Ross, can you tell us what you're feeling?"

All he could do was shake his head. Marlena sat quietly showing little emotion but she was wondering what was going on inside him. She knew, from her own sessions, that something was about to happen. She had had enough therapy to know that tears of this nature meant a breakthrough was coming. She was very, very hopeful.

"Ross, what's going on in there?" The therapist also saw the tears as a good sign but was anticipating an abrupt exit on Ross' part.

"I just...need a minute," he mustered.

"We'll give you some time. Speak when you feel you're ready," she said.

Time, Marlena thought. *He always needs time. How much more time will you need, Ross? You've had lots of time*, she thought and let out a barely audible sigh of frustration.

"Marlena, we'll start with you then," said the therapist hesitantly. She knew that there was a chance of losing Ross if she didn't get him to verbalize what he was feeling in that moment. She prompted Marlena because she knew she couldn't afford total silence in the room without running the risk of losing everyone else; especially Abrie. But before Marlena could begin, Ross blurted out, "I can't make it make sense."

Holding up her hand, palm out, as a motion to stop Marlena, the therapist asked, "What, Ross. You can't make what make sense?"

"This whole thing," he blurted out. "Nothing in my life makes sense anymore."

"Well, let's see if we can make some of it come together. When you said that, what was the most pressing thing on your mind?"

"What do you mean?" he asked.

"You know—job, car, house, marriage, relationships? What do you think about the most?"

"Abrie. Why did this have to happen to Abrie? She was such a brilliant and vibrant girl, so full of life and a good kid. Why did this have to happen to her?"

Marlena's heart sank. She was hoping he would address their relationship. She was hoping she was the most pressing issue for him. That would have made her the most important thing in his life, but as she suspected, it was Abrie. But go figure. That was the most important thing in Reggie's life, too. Her sons were also more concerned about Abrie than they were her. Abrie, Abrie, Abrie. Everything was always about Abrie and before she knew it, she had blurted it out-- much to the surprise of the therapist, but certainly not to Ross. Marlena's selfishness was no shock to Ross at all.

"Abrie, Abrie, Abrie. That's all you ever think about. That's all you've ever cared about...," she snorted.

"Well, someone had to think about her because it sure wasn't going to be the chief coroner. All she thinks about is dead bodies; primarily the one of Reggie Lofton," he snapped.

"Now that was low. You didn't have to go there," she hissed through clenched teeth.

"Sure I had to go there. That's the only place any of us can find you; in the graveyard of your mind, babysitting Reggie's dead body," he said to antagonize her.

"What about your precious Bianca, who was so royal that no one could even know about for fear of them speaking her name?"

"You're right. Bianca was precious and I tried to make you the same but you kept rejecting my advances. I tried to make up for it through giving you what I should have given to her, but what I got in return was what you probably should have given to Reggie; the cold shoulder."

"What do you mean you tried to 'make her the same'?" the therapist asked for redirection.

"I tried to treat Marlena like I treated Bianca. I wanted to give her what I never got the chance to give Bianca, but she never, ever accepted it. For years I couldn't see where I had gone wrong, and I still don't see it. Why couldn't my wife just be a wife and accept what I had to give her? Why did she have to be so cold?"

"Perhaps part of the problem was that what you were trying to give to her belonged to someone else. Things may have gone bad, Ross, when you tried to make Marlena Bianca in your mind," she said supportively.

"Yep. I knew it," Marlena contended. "And all these years, you tried to blame me..."

"Wait a minute, Marlena. You are certainly not innocent here."

"I beg your pardon. Just what's that supposed to mean?"

"It means that both of you are at least guilty of trying to keep your lates alive through each other, and that wasn't fair to either of you. Marrying Ross was not supposed to be a second chance at Reggie and," she continued as she turned to Ross, "marrying Marlena was not a second chance at making things right for Bianca. However," she said with a pause, "if you play your cards right, you can have a second chance at being married to one another."

Ross turned and stared out the window, exhibiting body language that suggested uncertainty about taking that chance. Marlena sat motionless. Abrie was playing with the armguards on her chair. She was obviously unaware of what was now going on around her, which was probably a good thing.

After a few moments of silence, the therapist threw out a question. "Do you think this marriage is repairable?"

After a long pause, Marlena began to speak. "I think with a lot of work, we can put things back together. I think if we start on the right foot this time, we could build a marriage that will be even better than the one before."

"'Better than the one before,'" Ross scoffed. "Anything is better than the one before."

"Ross," the therapist said, "it's obvious that you're angry, so why don't you just tell Marlena that rather than throwing daggers at her. We could get so much more done if you'd just address the issue rather than poking around it. Look at her and tell her that you're angry. Then tell her why."

"That's silly," said Ross. "She knows I'm angry. I shouldn't have to tell her that. "

"Does she know why you're angry?"

"If she doesn't, there must be something wrong with her."

"It's a yes or no question, Ross. Does she know why you're angry with her?"

Ross wouldn't answer so the therapist posed the question to Marlena, "do you know why Ross is angry?"

"No. I really don't. I guess he's mad because I spent too much time at work. I guess..."

"You know exactly why I'm angry," he said sharply, cutting her off.

"No, Ross. I really don't know why you're angry. As a matter of fact, I'm not even sure *you* know why you're angry."

"I wouldn't be angry if you had treated me the way a wife should."

"So it's all my fault, huh, Ross? You're so innocent. I messed up the marriage by myself; all by myself? How is that possible?"

"Hold on, you two. We are not going to get anywhere like this. This is not a blaming session and we need to talk more civilly to one another."

"What we need to do is pray," Ross said under his breath.

"What was that, Ross?" the therapist asked.

"I said we need to pray because that's what was missing from the marriage the whole time. I used to pray before getting into this marriage and it seemed that I had answers or at least I had somewhere to go when I didn't know what to do, but it seems that over the last ten years, I have lost that. I've lost myself. I've lost my family. I've lost everything, and this happened because she refused to go to church. She refused to be a part of any and everything I was, and I gave it all up for her. I lost everything that meant anything to me because of her and if you want to know why I'm angry, there it is."

The room was so silent you could have heard a pin drop. No one had a comeback for that one because of the emotion in which Ross used to express himself. It threw everyone for a loop and the room stayed quiet for a few minutes until the therapist suggested they meet again.

"I thought we were going to discuss Abrie's release date," Marlena chimed in.

"We've got a little ways to go before her date actually comes up. Why don't we discuss that at a later time?"

"But don't we need to know that now?" Ross asked.

"My professional opinion is that we need to work on the issues that would hinder her progress before working on a release for her. It is absolutely imperative that the place she's released to makes her feel safe and secure; if not, you can almost be assured of a relapse and she's making too much progress for us to take that chance. Her release date will be determined after several factors are taken into consideration and the home environment is one of them. Are you thinking of taking her home in the midst of this turmoil? It would not be good for her and she is our main concern here."

The silence on the part of Ross and Marlena felt like humble submission. Neither of them was in a position to argue with the professional opinion of someone who'd just witnessed them acting like spoiled children.

Ross exited the front doors of the center shortly before Marlena, who came calling after him. He saw that her car was parked a couple of rows in front of his own. Sighing with his shoulders, he stopped and turned around to see what she wanted.

Running to catch up with him, she reached for his hand. He just looked at her with a blank stare. "Ross, Baby, let's talk. I don't want to fight anymore. I know things weren't as they should have been between us but this is crazy. I want you to come home. Please, if we can't do this for ourselves, let's do it for Abrie."

"Marlena, we've been over this a hundred times already. I don't want to talk about it and I don't want to come home. I'm fine where I am and I'm going to stay there until I get my thoughts together about what I'm going to do. When I'm ready to talk, we'll talk. What about this do you not understand?" he asked in a condescending tone.

"I don't understand why you're making this so difficult. I don't understand why you won't deal with this and I don't understand how you could just walk out of a ten year relationship and not look back. Honey, I love you!"

"Marlena, why did it take ten years for you to say that? Do you really love me or do you just want me to move back into the house? What do you need? A built-in babysitter for Abrie? What are you trying to get me to do for you this time? Your manipulating schemes worked for ten years but it's time you understand that you ain't got it like that no more," he said in his best street tone.

"Ross, what do I have to do to get you to at least discuss this with me?"

"We *are* discussing it. What you really need to do is leave me alone until I'm ready to talk. Stop pushing me because I'm tired of being pushed around by you. The days of that are finally, *finally* over."

"Ross, we need to handle this as mature adults. We have a child who needs us and all you can think about is yourself," she blurted out of sheer desperation.

"I can't believe that you, of all people, said that. I'll call you later," he mumbled and began walking to his car, leaving her standing in the parking lot. Marlena found herself watching his back get farther and farther away from her when she heard herself say something she hadn't said in at least ten years. She felt a slight rumbling through her body as she said, "maybe he's right. We do need to pray."

THIRTY-SIX

Now that the swelling was completely gone, Della was using her hand to do things she hadn't done in a while. It's funny how you take things for granted until something bad makes you aware of its importance, she thought to herself. As she put down the last potted plant, the phone rang.

"Hello."

"Hi Del. It's me, Nancy."

"Oh, hey girl. I heard you called a couple of days ago. Are you back in town yet?"

"No, but I'll be there sometime tomorrow evening. How are you feeling? I hear strange creatures have been feasting on you."

After a light chuckle, Della replied, "Yeah, and I must be pretty tasty because that little joker tried to eat me alive. How are things going with your parents?"

"Pretty well, thanks. God gave me some good ones, if I may say so myself. We've been hanging out and doing lots of things together. All I can say is that I hope to be that much in love with my husband after three and a half decades of marriage. They are like two turtledoves."

"Yeah, me, too. And speaking of marriage, Abraham proposed to me the other day. I couldn't believe it," she said with a shriek. "Personally, I think he's just in shock after having almost lost me to the bug world."

"Hey, that's cool," Nancy mustered. "What did you say?"

"Funny you should ask. Most people assume I just said 'yes' but I didn't. I told him we hadn't been together long enough to even consider marriage and that we should revisit the idea in a couple of years."

"Wow, Del. That was pretty mature," Nancy said surprised. "I don't know if I could have done that."

"That's because you've never been married before. We veterans know that it takes more than fairytale love, lust and a couple of 'I - do's' to make a real marriage work. I know that there needs to be something deeper than what we feel for each other right now to make that kind of move. Honestly, I think he's just fascinated with the idea of me. He needs more time to get to know the things about me that I'm hiding from him right now; like the fact that I tend to ingest a whole lot more in one sitting than he's ever seen me eat," she laughed.

Laughing too, Nancy said, "Oh, so you're taking the princess-sized bites right now, huh?"

"You got it. Well, I need to get some things done around the house before it gets too late. You did say you were coming in tomorrow evening, right?"

"Yep. Sure did."

"Nance, let's have dinner together for old time sake."

"Yeah, it's been a while, hasn't it? But what about Abraham?"

"Yes, it's been a while and I think I'm a big girl. I don't need Abraham to be with me as I eat my dinner."

"I've got just one question before we go."

"What's that?"

"If I pay, will you still eat princess-sized bites, or will I have to dig out my gold card to pay for your meal?" Both ladies got a real good laugh off that one before hanging up the phone.

Nancy lied down on the bed in the guest room of her parent's house and decided to do some reflecting. She had the house all to herself due to a mandatory board meeting at her father's church. She was remembering the conversation she'd had with her father the night before, and how it had all come about. To her surprise, he brought up the ordeal that had taken place at his church all those years ago. He talked about how it had affected him, and the fact that there wasn't much he could do to help her understand it since she was so young. He had discussed it with her mother, who suggested he leave it alone and just pray about it. In her infinite wisdom, she knew things would be okay in time.

Nancy was able to discuss with him her "affair of the heart" with Ross, which made her feel so much better. She and her father had had a second chance to talk about what happens when a married man is faced with dealing with the affection of a woman who is not his wife. They talked about how it could be rather flattering, but no more than a trap of the enemy.

They also discussed how crucial the first response of the flattered is: if it is inviting, it could mean an affair, which would inevitably cause damage to the marriage and a lot of pain to a lot of people. If it's handled appropriately, there's still the risk of someone getting hurt, but, if dealt with tactfully, the marriage would be left intact.

That long awaited conversation went well and Nancy knew that it had because of the kind of man her father was. He was smooth and knew how to handle himself in any situation. She kicked herself for not understanding then what she understood now. Her father was a good man and she should have known that. But it was finally out in the open and she could let go of it. Her father warned her of the dangers of getting involved with a married man and, of the many pieces of advice he had given her, one stood out from the rest. He suggested that before even considering getting involved with a married man, a woman should take a long hard look at the problem or problems his wife had to be dealing with concerning him and whether or not *he'd* brought them into the marriage with *him*. Aside from the fact that it was totally wrong, no matter how you looked at it, what kind of demons would she be inviting into her life?

She had never thought about it in that way because she'd always seen Ross as having been so perfect. It never occurred to her that Ross could have been, and probably was, a part of the problem. She smiled to herself and basked in the gratitude she had for having been able to reunite with a man as wonderful a man as her father before it was too late.

Della on the other hand, left the stand where her phone was placed, walked over to her couch, and sat down. She looked long and hard at the manila envelope Abraham had left with her and asked her not to open. She didn't know exactly what it was, but she did have a feeling and wondered why he had involved her in that way. She picked up the envelope, carried it into her room with her and, after moving some things around, deposited it into a safe place in her home that no one else knew about. Not even the author of this book. As for Marlena and Ross? Well, you be the judge of that.